Schaumburg Township District Library
130 South Roselle Road
Schaumburg, Illinois 60193

GAYLORD

THE PHANTOM
OF THE OPERA

Adapted by

Joeming Dunn

Illustrated by

Rod Espinosa

Based upon the works of

Gaston Leroux

magic
Wagon

visit us at
www.abdopublishing.com

Published by Magic Wagon, a division of the ABDO Group, 8000 West 78th Street, Edina, Minnesota 55439. Copyright © 2010 by Abdo Consulting Group, Inc. International copyrights reserved in all countries. All rights reserved. No part of this book may be reproduced in any form without written permission from the publisher.

Graphic Planet™ is a trademark and logo of Magic Wagon.

Printed in the United States.

♻ Manufactured with paper containing at least 10% post-consumer waste

Original novel by Gaston Leroux
Adapted by Joeming Dunn
Illustrated, colored and lettered by Rod Espinosa
Edited by Stephanie Hedlund and Rochelle Baltzer
Interior layout and design by Antarctic Press
Cover art by Ben Dunn
Cover design by Neil Klinepier

Library of Congress Cataloging-in-Publication Data

Dunn, Joeming W.
    The Phantom of the Opera / Gaston Leroux; adapted by Joeming Dunn and illustrated by Rod Espinosa ; based upon the works of Gaston Leroux.
    p. cm. -- (Graphic planet. Graphic horror)
    ISBN 978-1-60270-679-8 (alk. paper)
    1. Graphic novels. [1. Graphic novels. 2. Leroux, Gaston, 1868-1927. Fantôme de l'Opéra--Adaptations. 3. Paris (France)--History--1870-1940--Fiction. 4. France--History--Third Republic, 1870-1940--Fiction. 5. Horror stories.] I. Espinosa, Rod, ill. II. Leroux, Gaston, 1868-1927. Fantôme de l'Opéra. English. III. Title.

PZ7.7.D86Ph 2010
741.5'973--dc22

                                                                2009008606

TABLE OF CONTENTS

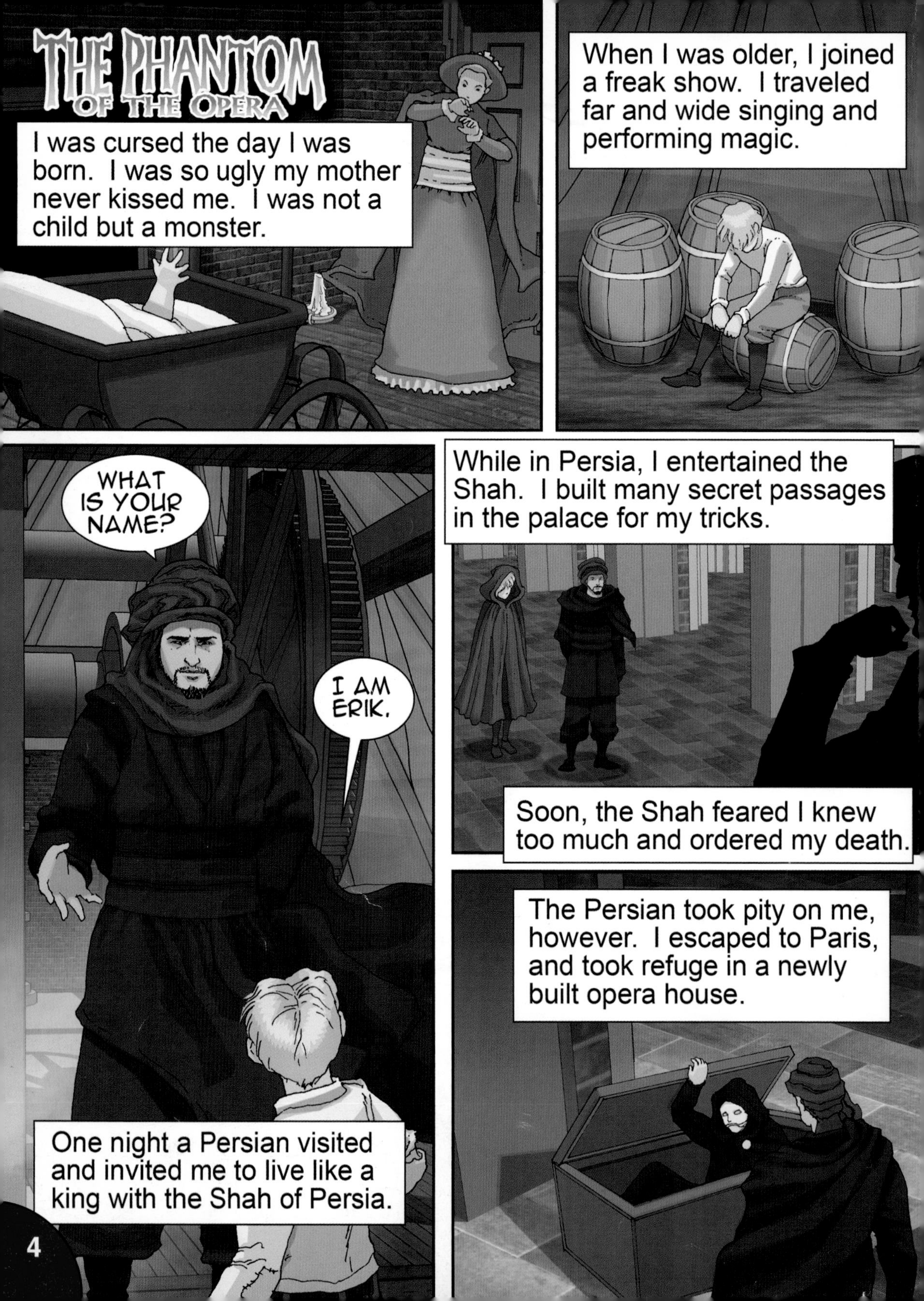

THE PHANTOM OF THE OPERA
I was cursed the day I was born. I was so ugly my mother never kissed me. I was not a child but a monster.
When I was older, I joined a freak show. I traveled far and wide singing and performing magic.
WHAT IS YOUR NAME?
I AM ERIK.
One night a Persian visited and invited me to live like a king with the Shah of Persia.
While in Persia, I entertained the Shah. I built many secret passages in the palace for my tricks.
Soon, the Shah feared I knew too much and ordered my death.
The Persian took pity on me, however. I escaped to Paris, and took refuge in a newly built opera house.

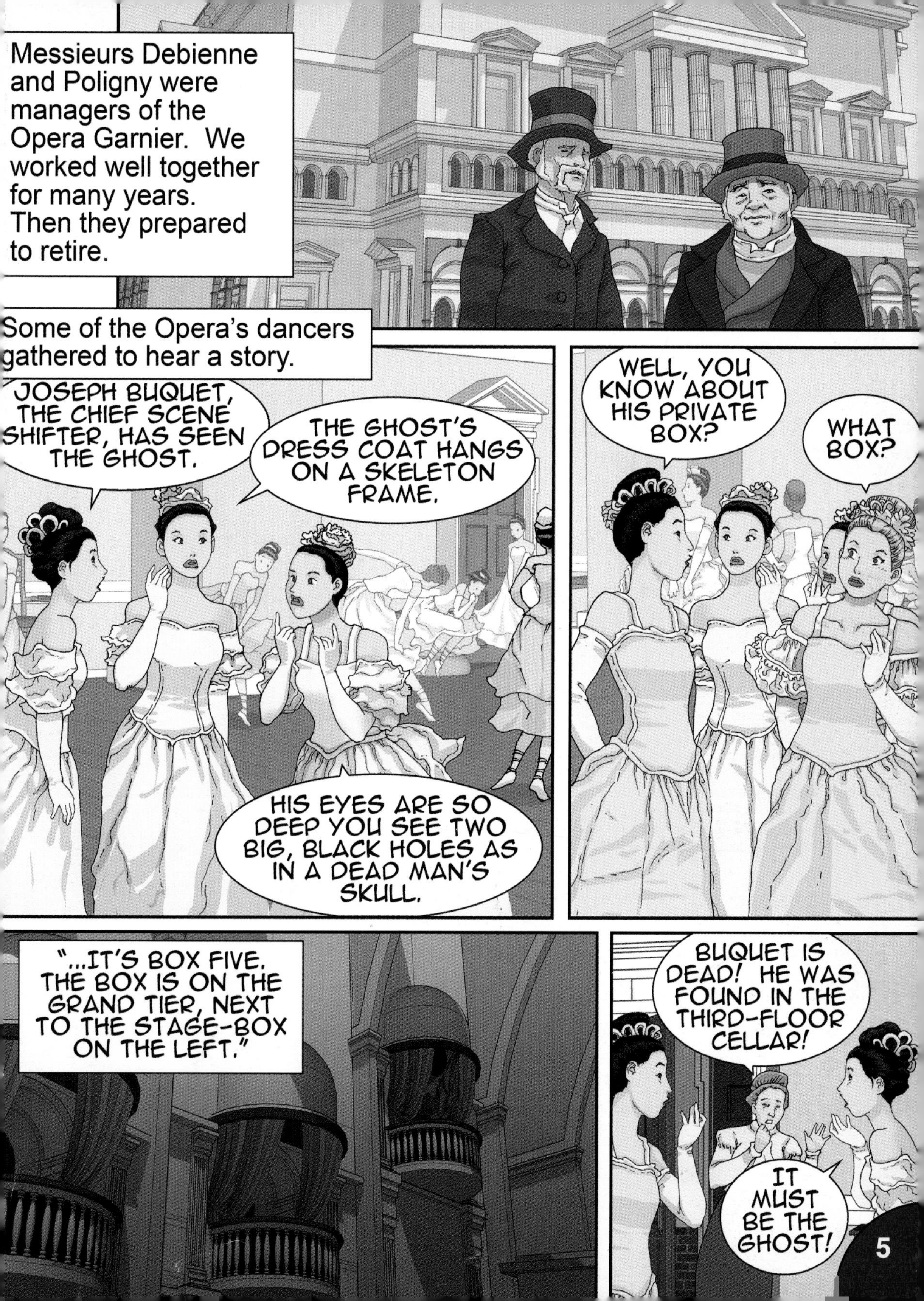
Messieurs Debienne and Poligny were managers of the Opera Garnier. We worked well together for many years. Then they prepared to retire.
Some of the Opera's dancers gathered to hear a story.
JOSEPH BUQUET, THE CHIEF SCENE SHIFTER, HAS SEEN THE GHOST.
THE GHOST'S DRESS COAT HANGS ON A SKELETON FRAME.
HIS EYES ARE SO DEEP YOU SEE TWO BIG, BLACK HOLES AS IN A DEAD MAN'S SKULL.
WELL, YOU KNOW ABOUT HIS PRIVATE BOX?
WHAT BOX?
"...IT'S BOX FIVE. THE BOX IS ON THE GRAND TIER, NEXT TO THE STAGE-BOX ON THE LEFT."
BUQUET IS DEAD! HE WAS FOUND IN THE THIRD-FLOOR CELLAR!
IT MUST BE THE GHOST!

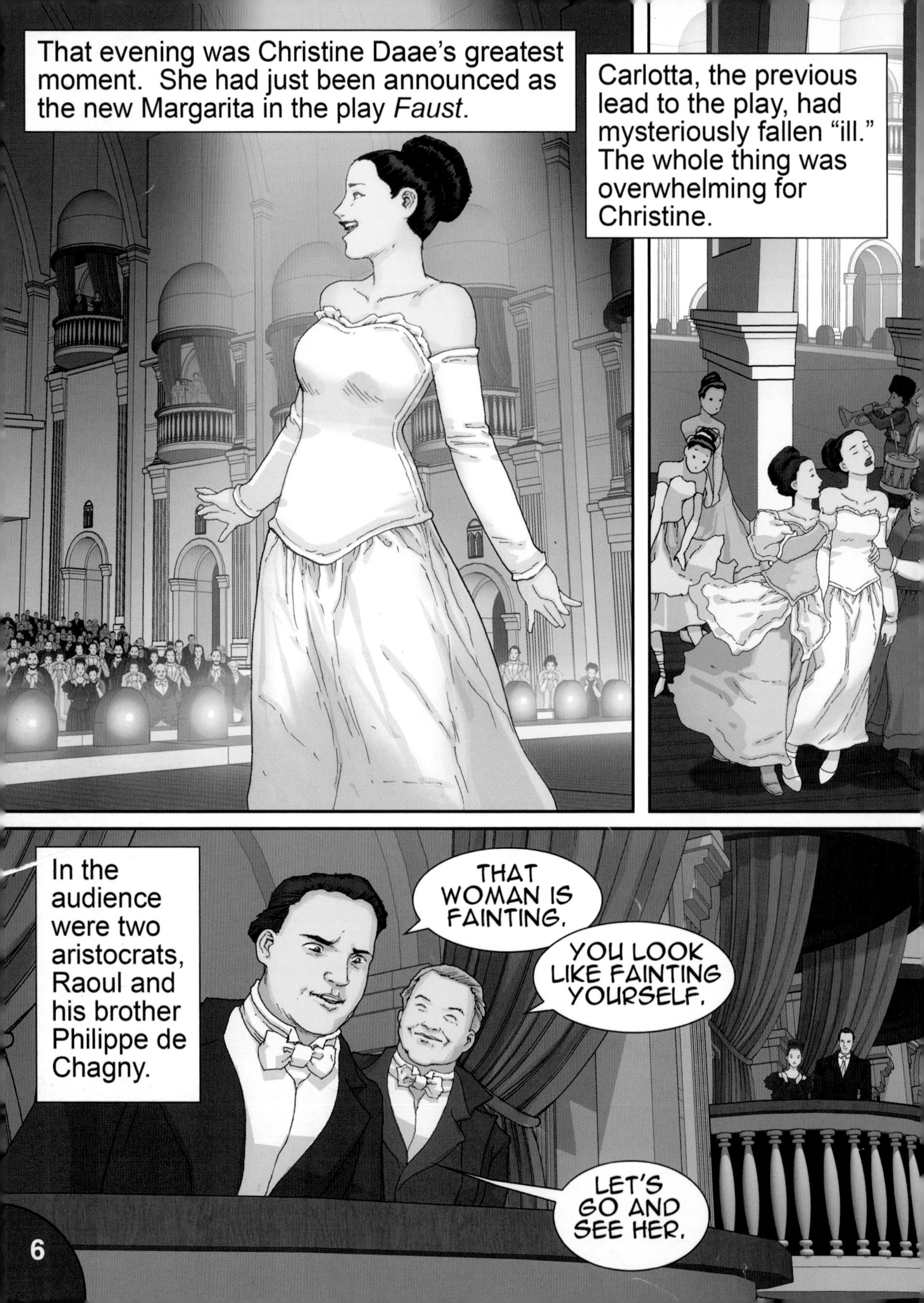
That evening was Christine Daae's greatest moment. She had just been announced as the new Margarita in the play *Faust*.
Carlotta, the previous lead to the play, had mysteriously fallen "ill." The whole thing was overwhelming for Christine.
In the audience were two aristocrats, Raoul and his brother Philippe de Chagny.
THAT WOMAN IS FAINTING.
YOU LOOK LIKE FAINTING YOURSELF.
LET'S GO AND SEE HER.

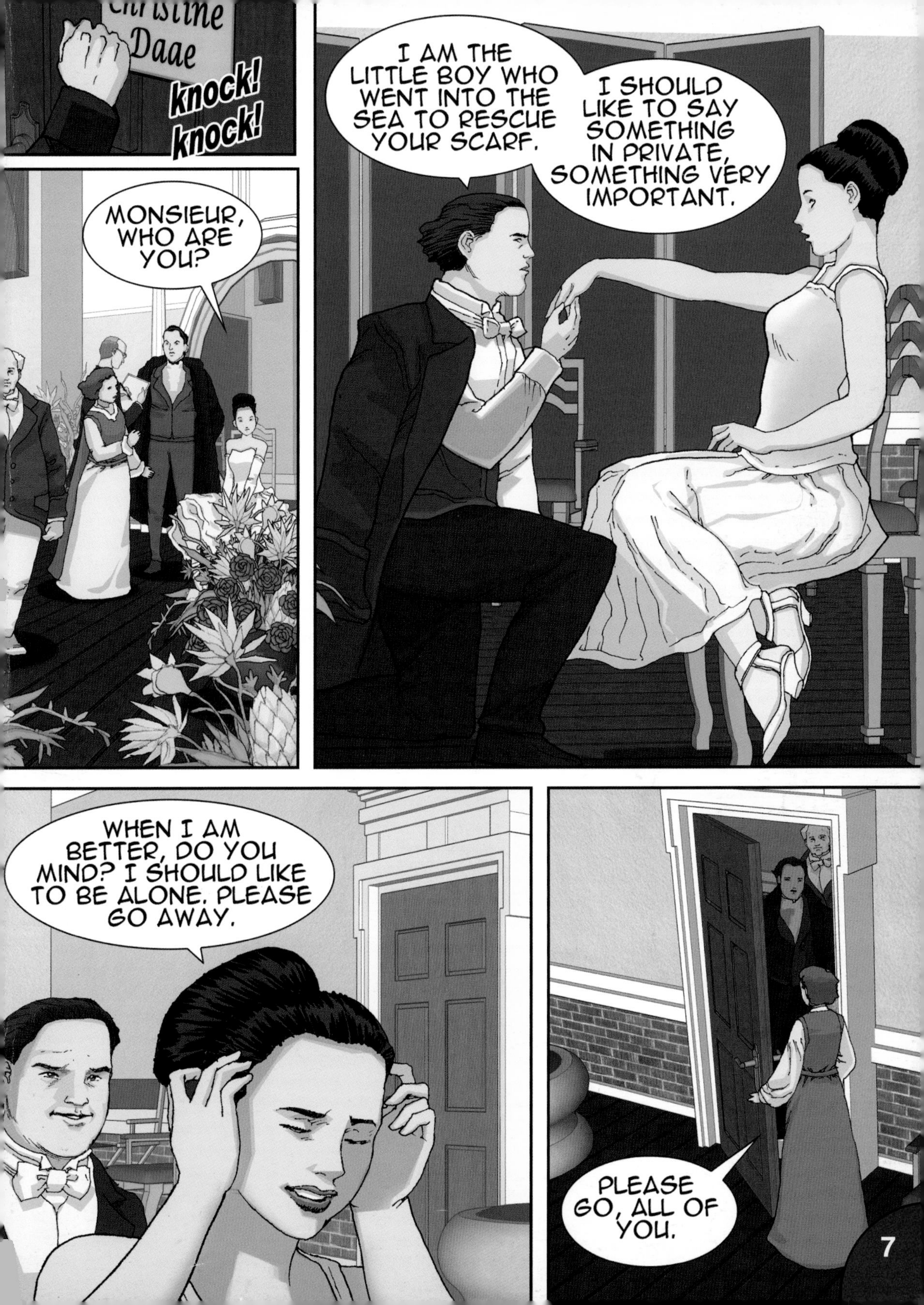
Christine Daae
knock! knock!
MONSIEUR, WHO ARE YOU?
I AM THE LITTLE BOY WHO WENT INTO THE SEA TO RESCUE YOUR SCARF.
I SHOULD LIKE TO SAY SOMETHING IN PRIVATE, SOMETHING VERY IMPORTANT.
WHEN I AM BETTER, DO YOU MIND? I SHOULD LIKE TO BE ALONE. PLEASE GO AWAY.
PLEASE GO, ALL OF YOU.

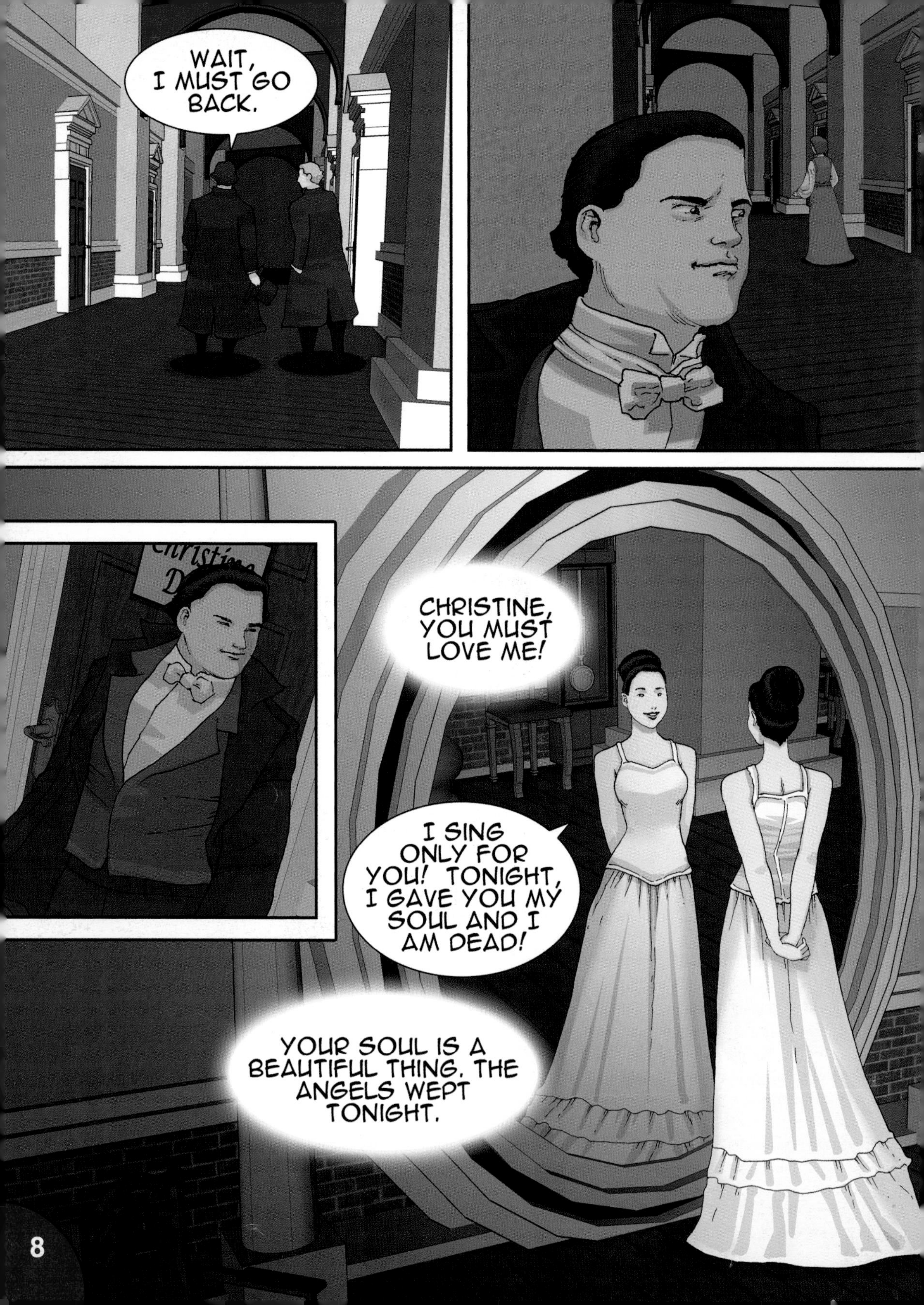
WAIT, I MUST GO BACK.
Christine D
CHRISTINE, YOU MUST LOVE ME!
I SING ONLY FOR YOU! TONIGHT, I GAVE YOU MY SOUL AND I AM DEAD!
YOUR SOUL IS A BEAUTIFUL THING. THE ANGELS WEPT TONIGHT.

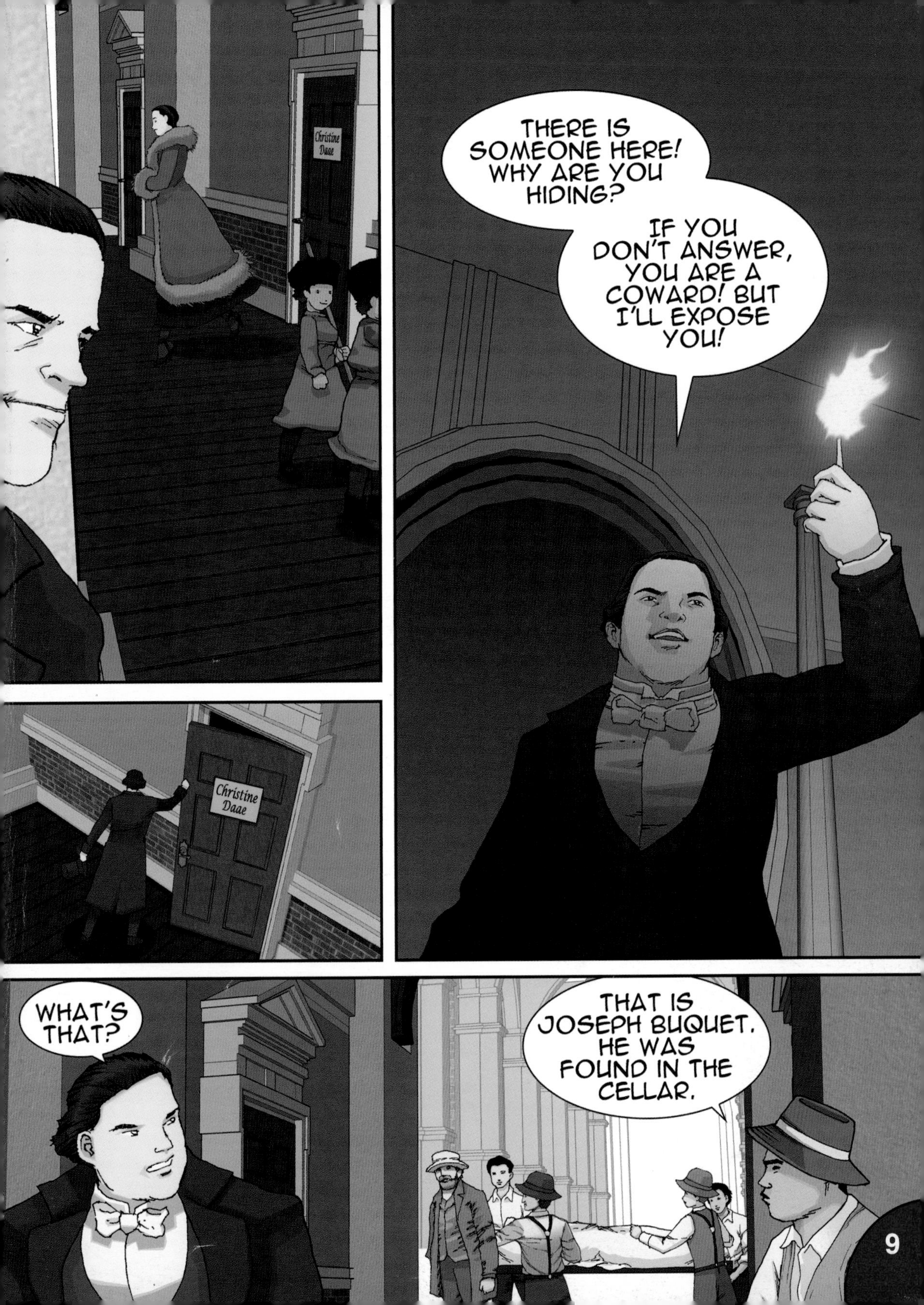

Christine Daae
Christine Daae
THERE IS SOMEONE HERE! WHY ARE YOU HIDING?
IF YOU DON'T ANSWER, YOU ARE A COWARD! BUT I'LL EXPOSE YOU!
WHAT'S THAT?
THAT IS JOSEPH BUQUET. HE WAS FOUND IN THE CELLAR.

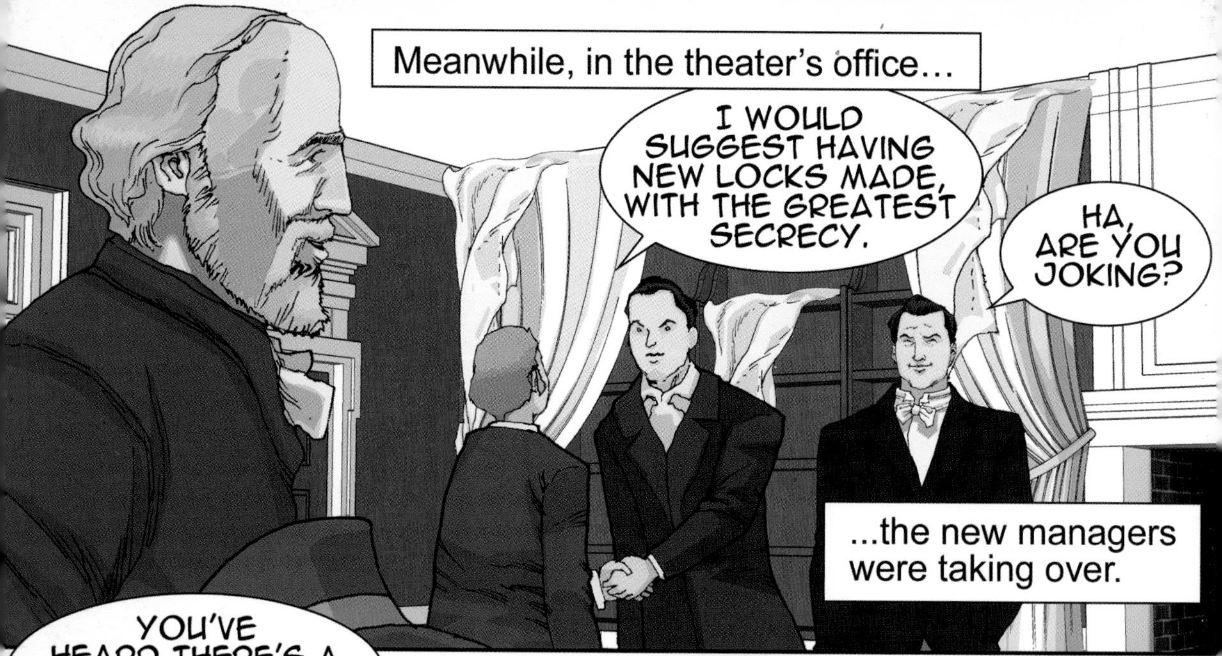
Meanwhile, in the theater's office…
I WOULD SUGGEST HAVING NEW LOCKS MADE, WITH THE GREATEST SECRECY.
HA, ARE YOU JOKING?
...the new managers were taking over.

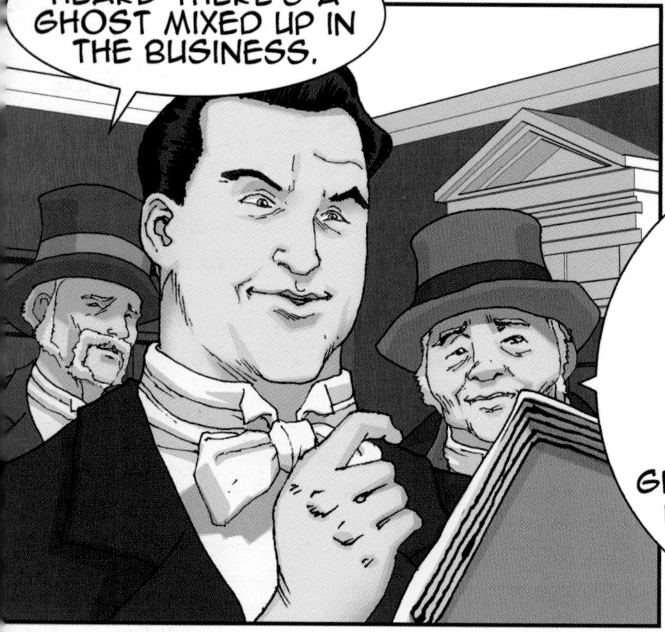
YOU'VE HEARD THERE'S A GHOST MIXED UP IN THE BUSINESS.

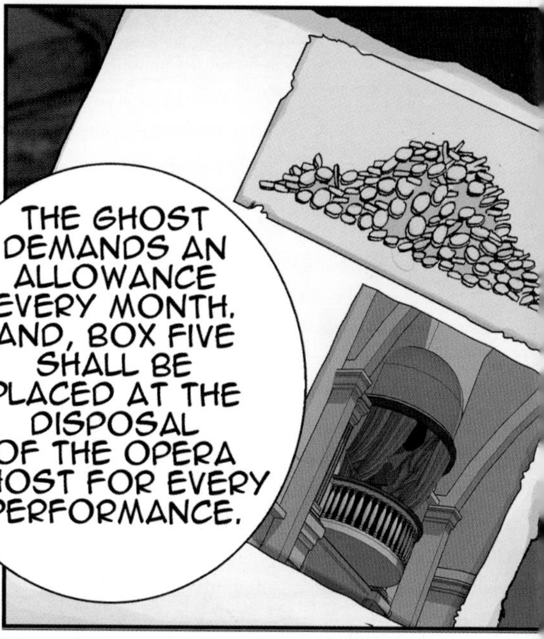
THE GHOST DEMANDS AN ALLOWANCE EVERY MONTH. AND, BOX FIVE SHALL BE PLACED AT THE DISPOSAL OF THE OPERA GHOST FOR EVERY PERFORMANCE.

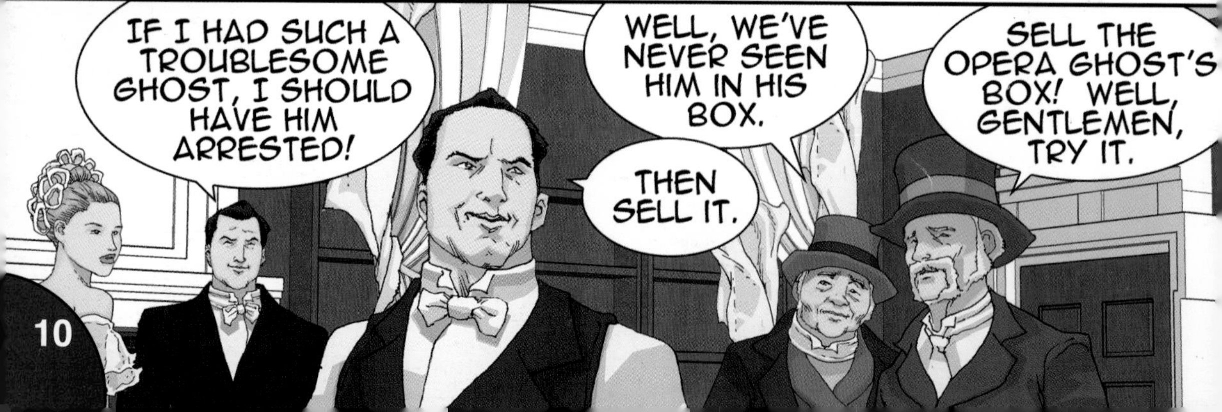
IF I HAD SUCH A TROUBLESOME GHOST, I SHOULD HAVE HIM ARRESTED!
WELL, WE'VE NEVER SEEN HIM IN HIS BOX.
THEN SELL IT.
SELL THE OPERA GHOST'S BOX! WELL, GENTLEMEN, TRY IT.

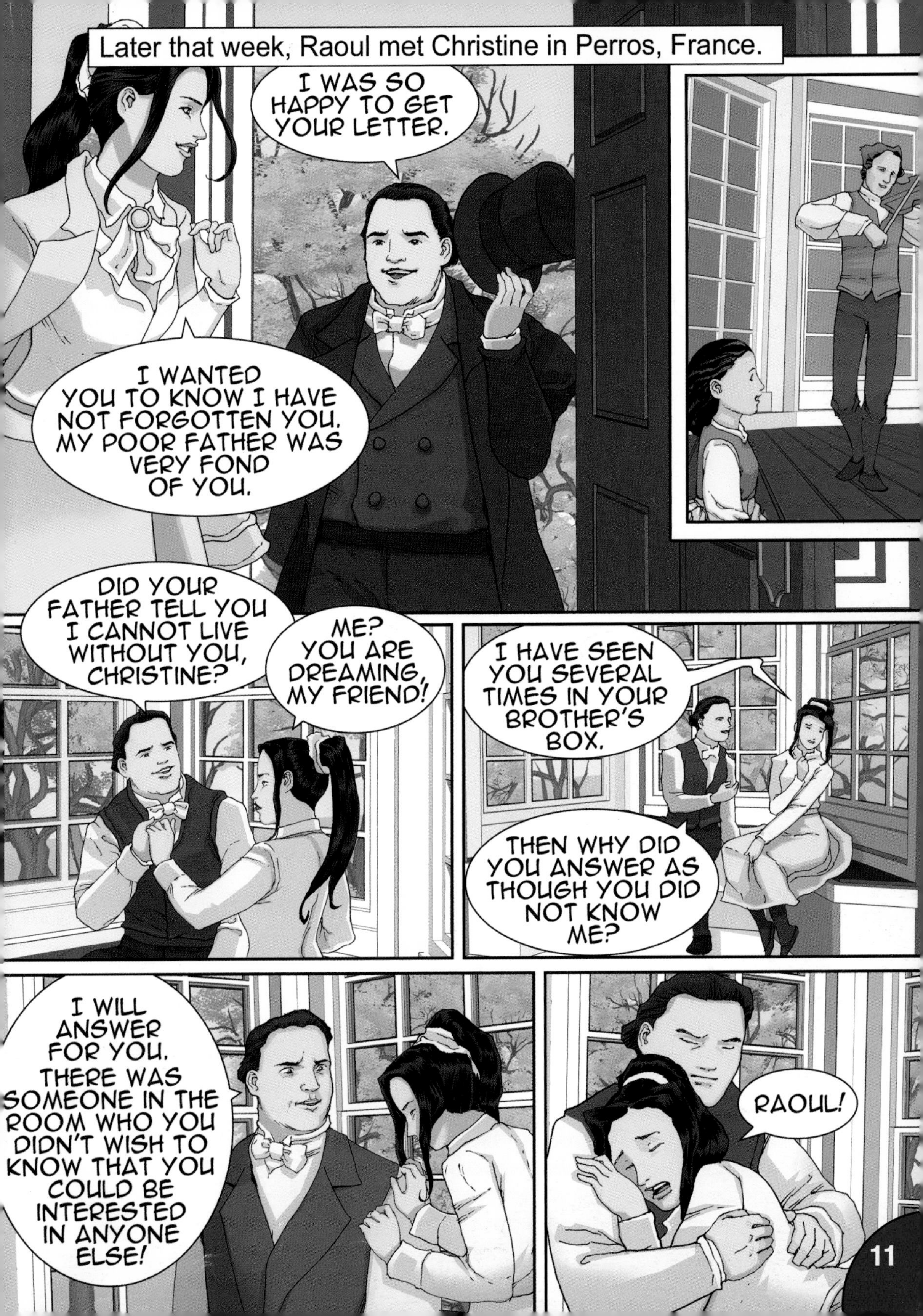
Later that week, Raoul met Christine in Perros, France.
I WAS SO HAPPY TO GET YOUR LETTER.
I WANTED YOU TO KNOW I HAVE NOT FORGOTTEN YOU. MY POOR FATHER WAS VERY FOND OF YOU.
DID YOUR FATHER TELL YOU I CANNOT LIVE WITHOUT YOU, CHRISTINE?
ME? YOU ARE DREAMING, MY FRIEND!
I HAVE SEEN YOU SEVERAL TIMES IN YOUR BROTHER'S BOX.
THEN WHY DID YOU ANSWER AS THOUGH YOU DID NOT KNOW ME?
I WILL ANSWER FOR YOU. THERE WAS SOMEONE IN THE ROOM WHO YOU DIDN'T WISH TO KNOW THAT YOU COULD BE INTERESTED IN ANYONE ELSE!
RAOUL!

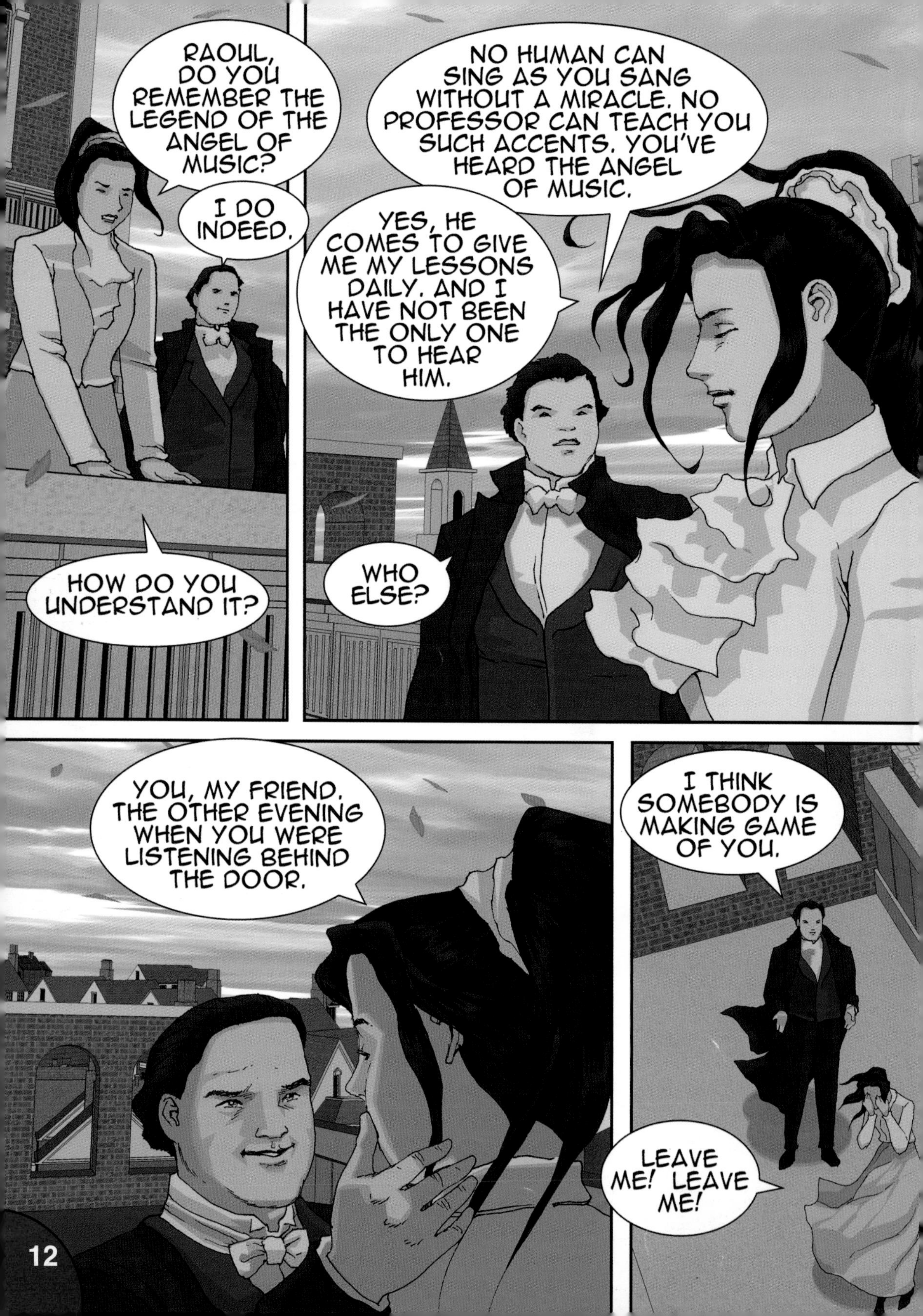
RAOUL, DO YOU REMEMBER THE LEGEND OF THE ANGEL OF MUSIC?
I DO INDEED.
HOW DO YOU UNDERSTAND IT?
NO HUMAN CAN SING AS YOU SANG WITHOUT A MIRACLE. NO PROFESSOR CAN TEACH YOU SUCH ACCENTS. YOU'VE HEARD THE ANGEL OF MUSIC.
YES, HE COMES TO GIVE ME MY LESSONS DAILY. AND I HAVE NOT BEEN THE ONLY ONE TO HEAR HIM.
WHO ELSE?
YOU, MY FRIEND. THE OTHER EVENING WHEN YOU WERE LISTENING BEHIND THE DOOR.
I THINK SOMEBODY IS MAKING GAME OF YOU.
LEAVE ME! LEAVE ME!

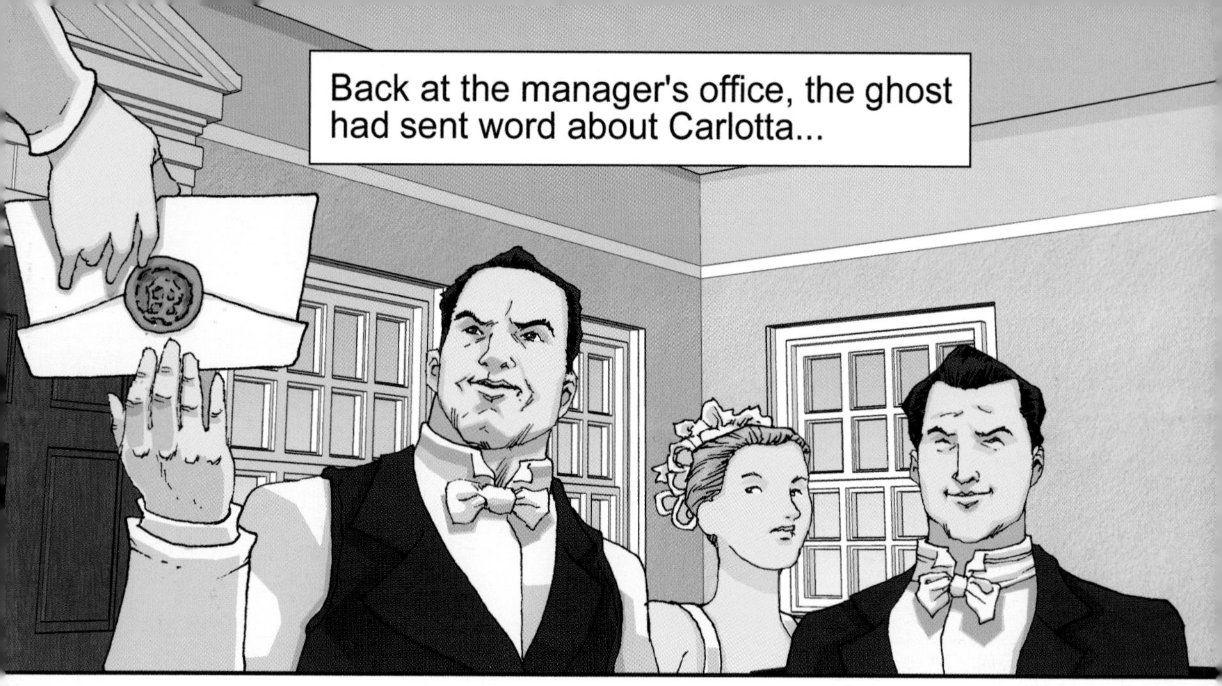
Back at the manager's office, the ghost had sent word about Carlotta...

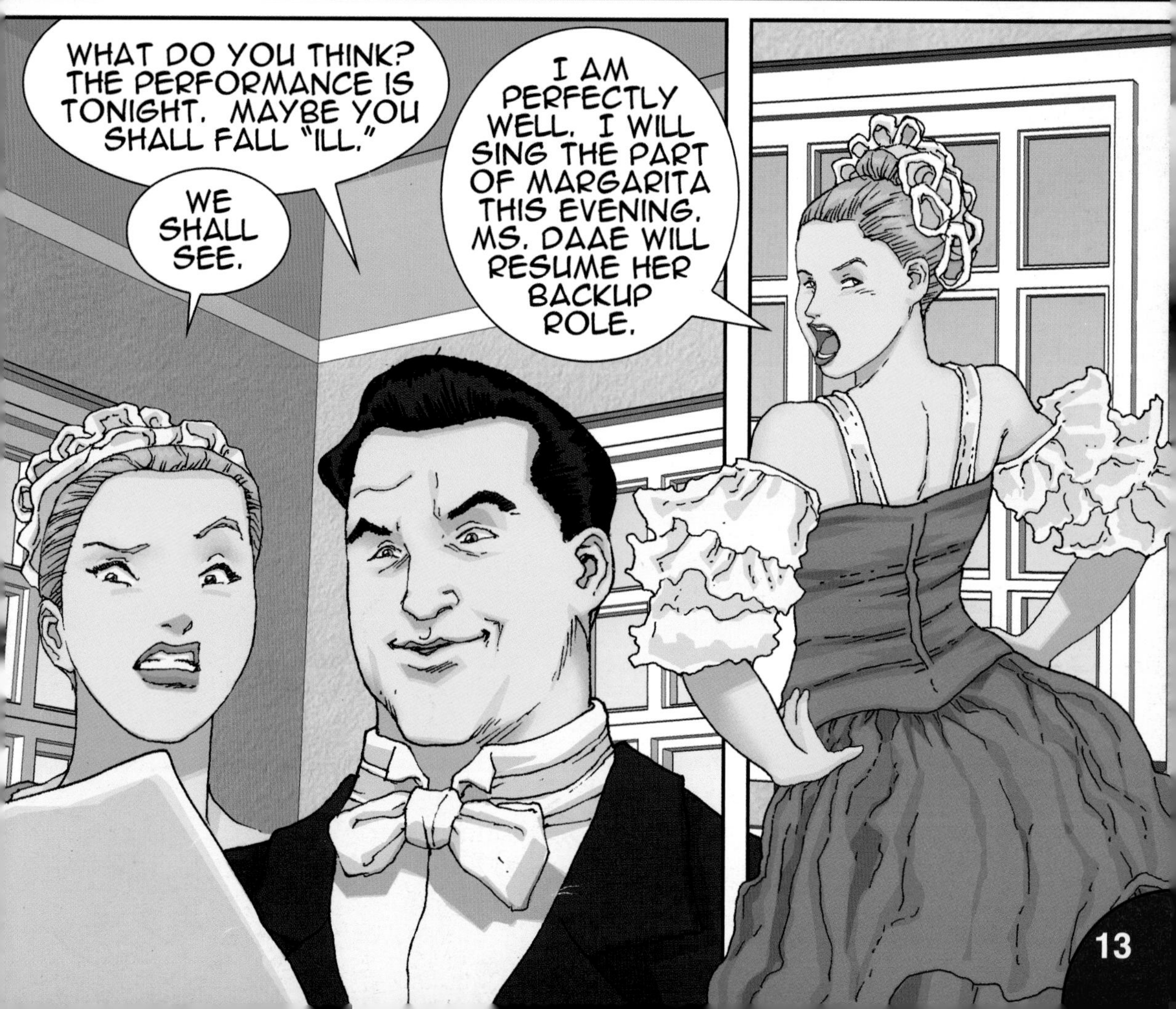
WHAT DO YOU THINK? THE PERFORMANCE IS TONIGHT. MAYBE YOU SHALL FALL "ILL."
WE SHALL SEE.
I AM PERFECTLY WELL. I WILL SING THE PART OF MARGARITA THIS EVENING. MS. DAAE WILL RESUME HER BACKUP ROLE.

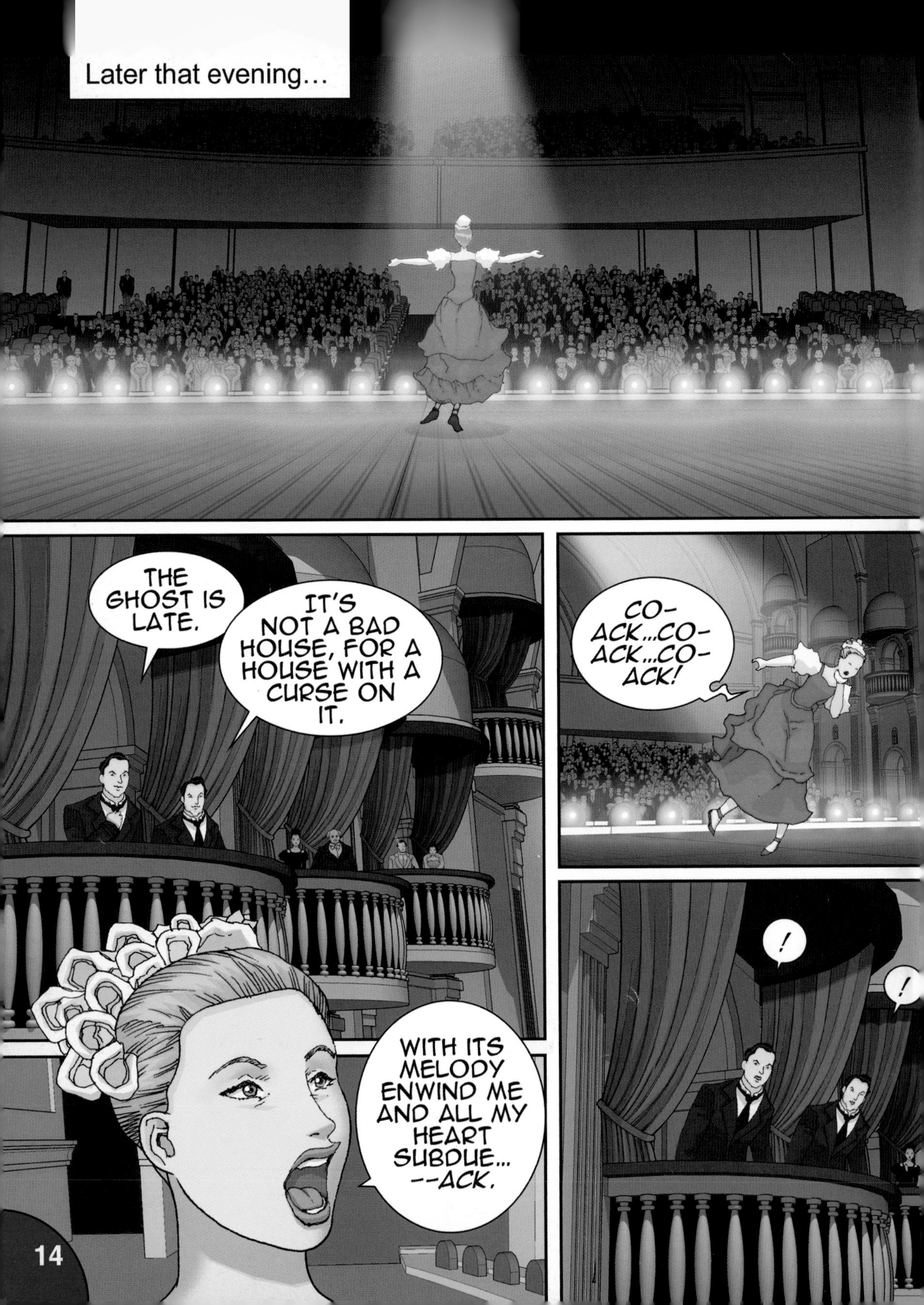
Later that evening…
THE GHOST IS LATE.
IT'S NOT A BAD HOUSE, FOR A HOUSE WITH A CURSE ON IT.
CO-ACK…CO-ACK…CO-ACK!
WITH ITS MELODY ENWIND ME AND ALL MY HEART SUBDUE… --ACK.
!
!

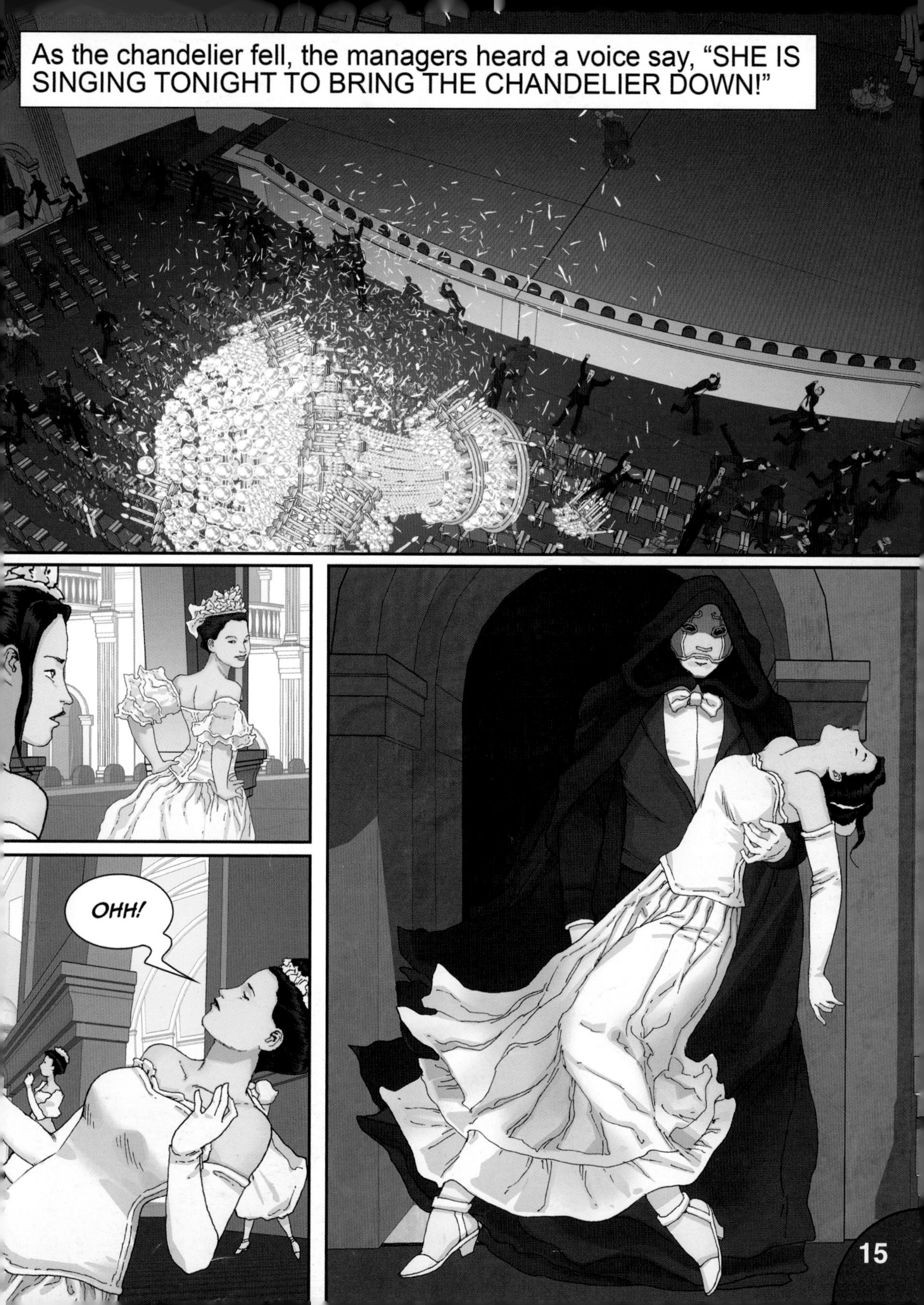
As the chandelier fell, the managers heard a voice say, "SHE IS SINGING TONIGHT TO BRING THE CHANDELIER DOWN!"
OHH!

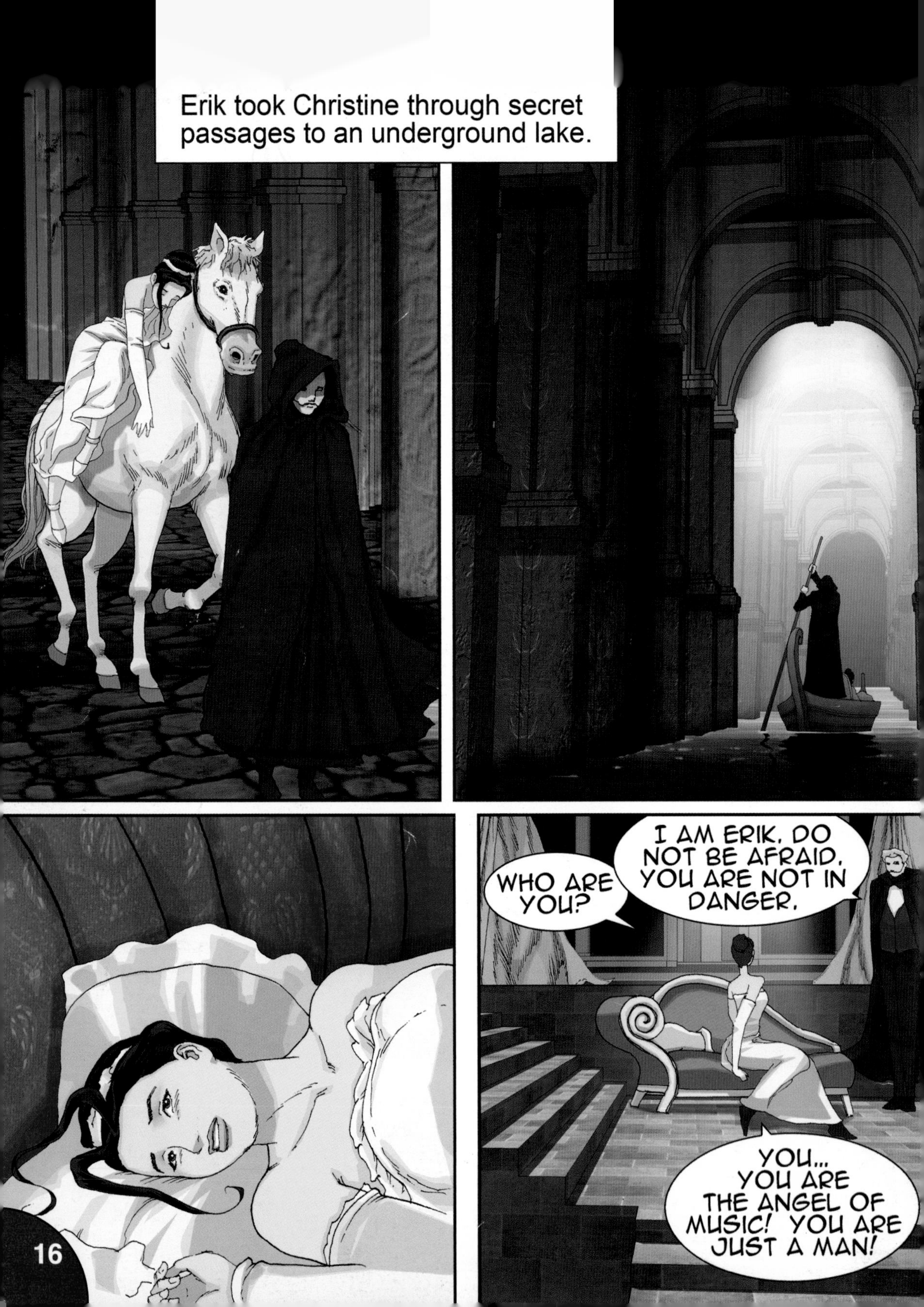
Erik took Christine through secret passages to an underground lake.
WHO ARE YOU?
I AM ERIK, DO NOT BE AFRAID. YOU ARE NOT IN DANGER.
YOU... YOU ARE THE ANGEL OF MUSIC! YOU ARE JUST A MAN!

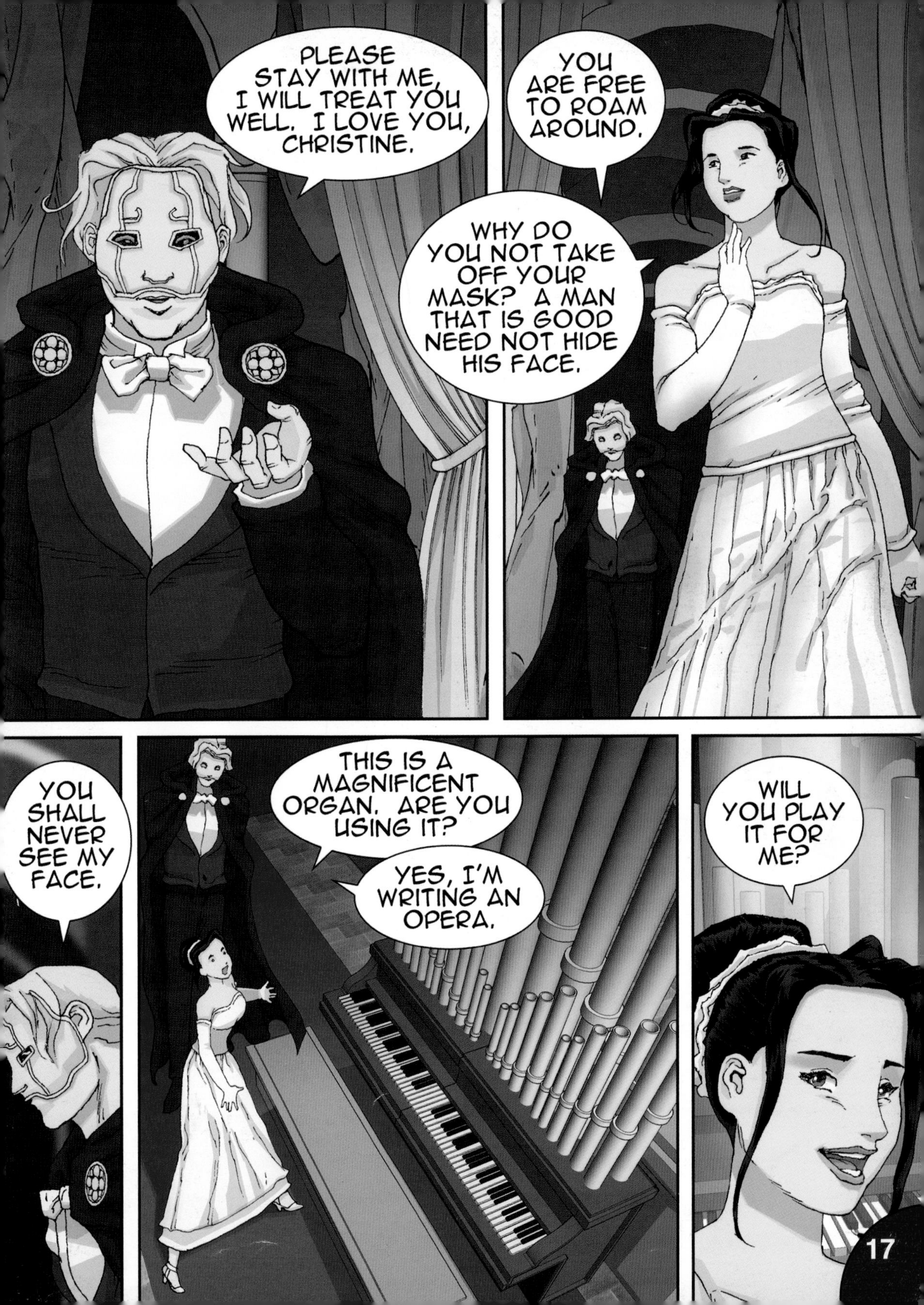
PLEASE STAY WITH ME, I WILL TREAT YOU WELL. I LOVE YOU, CHRISTINE.
YOU ARE FREE TO ROAM AROUND.
WHY DO YOU NOT TAKE OFF YOUR MASK? A MAN THAT IS GOOD NEED NOT HIDE HIS FACE.
YOU SHALL NEVER SEE MY FACE.
THIS IS A MAGNIFICENT ORGAN. ARE YOU USING IT?
YES, I'M WRITING AN OPERA.
WILL YOU PLAY IT FOR ME?

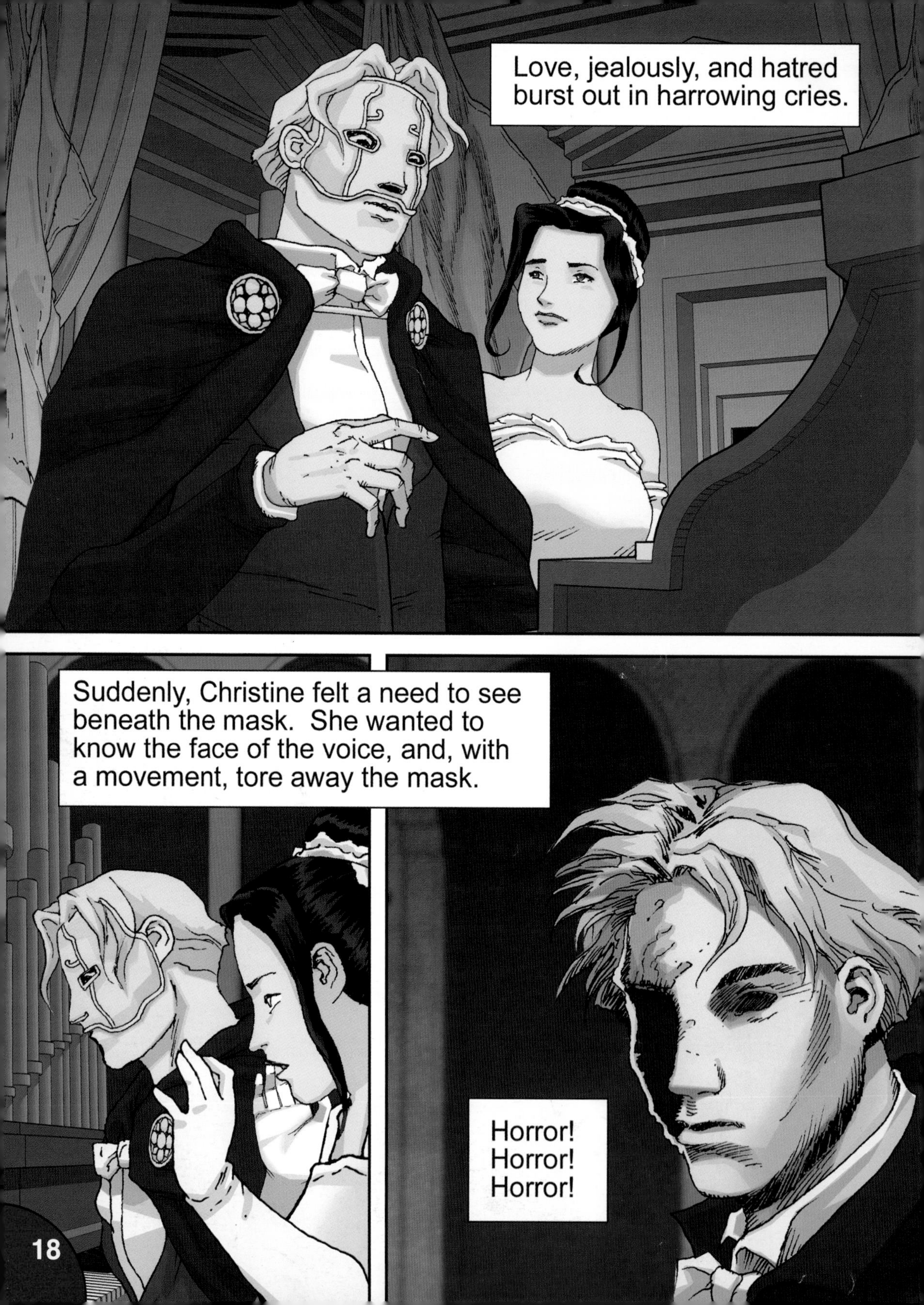
Love, jealously, and hatred burst out in harrowing cries.
Suddenly, Christine felt a need to see beneath the mask. She wanted to know the face of the voice, and, with a movement, tore away the mask.
Horror! Horror! Horror!

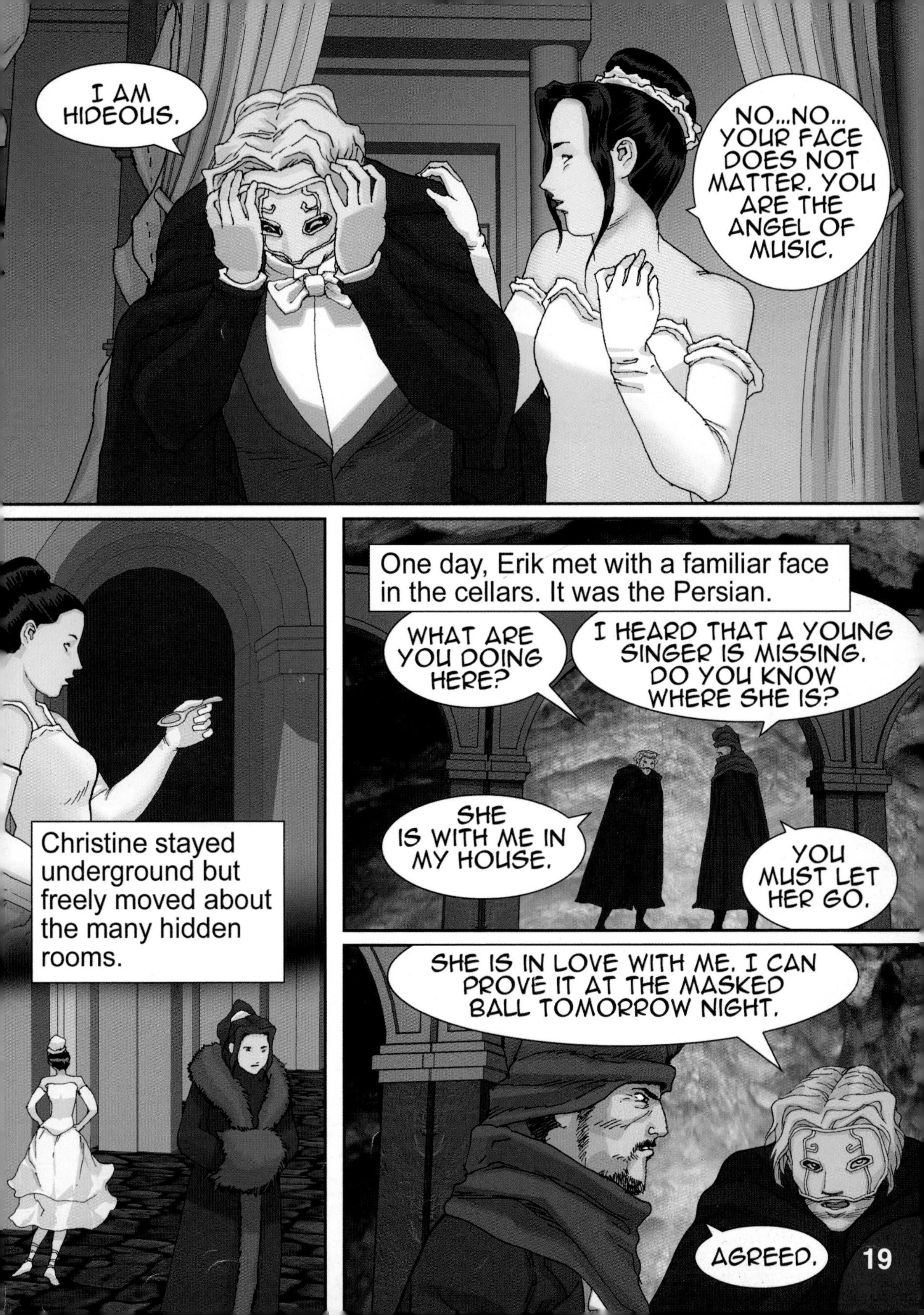

I AM HIDEOUS.
NO...NO... YOUR FACE DOES NOT MATTER. YOU ARE THE ANGEL OF MUSIC.
Christine stayed underground but freely moved about the many hidden rooms.
One day, Erik met with a familiar face in the cellars. It was the Persian.
WHAT ARE YOU DOING HERE?
I HEARD THAT A YOUNG SINGER IS MISSING. DO YOU KNOW WHERE SHE IS?
SHE IS WITH ME IN MY HOUSE.
YOU MUST LET HER GO.
SHE IS IN LOVE WITH ME. I CAN PROVE IT AT THE MASKED BALL TOMORROW NIGHT.
AGREED.

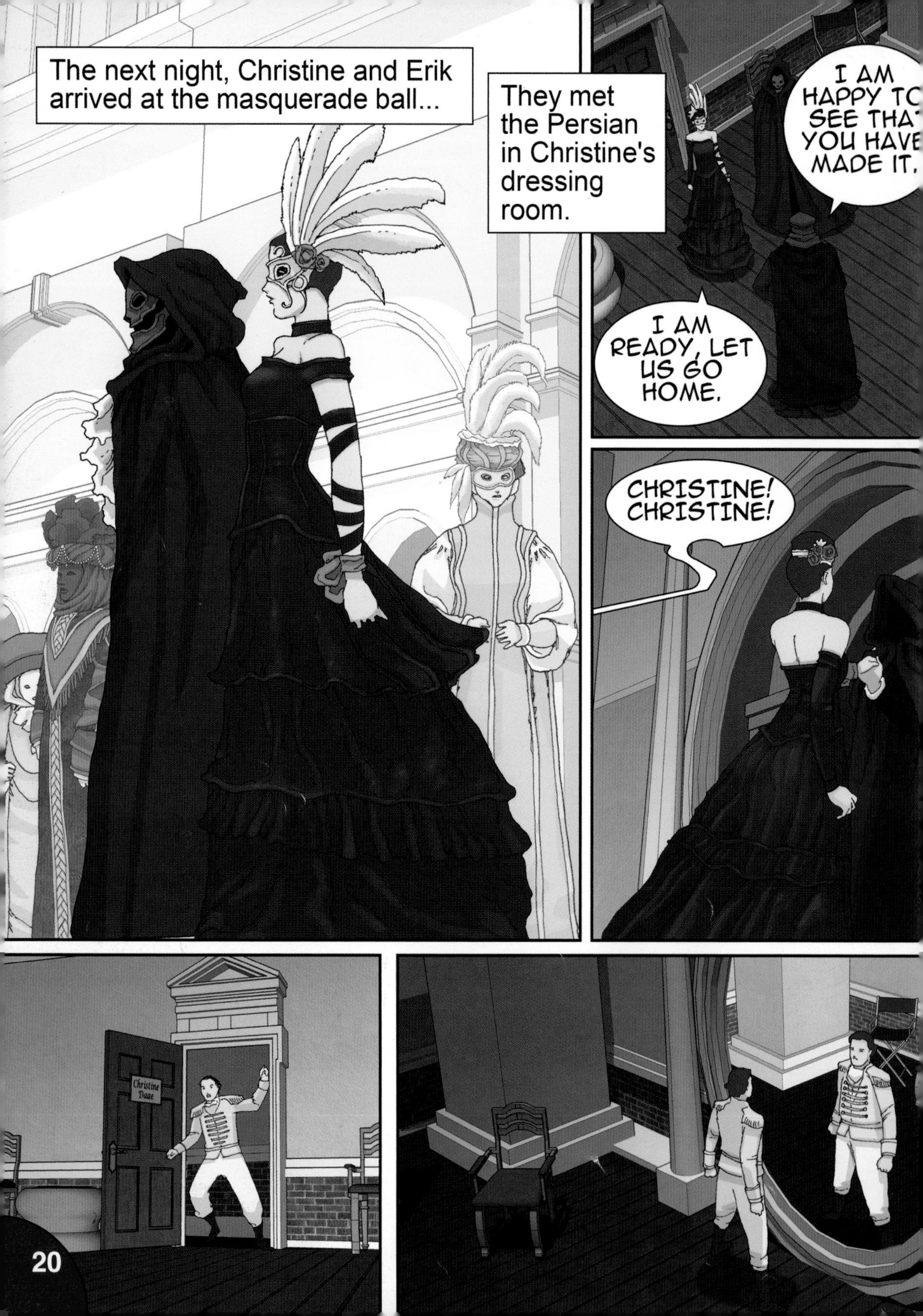

The next night, Christine and Erik arrived at the masquerade ball...
They met the Persian in Christine's dressing room.
I AM HAPPY TO SEE THAT YOU HAVE MADE IT.
I AM READY, LET US GO HOME.
CHRISTINE! CHRISTINE!
Christine Daae

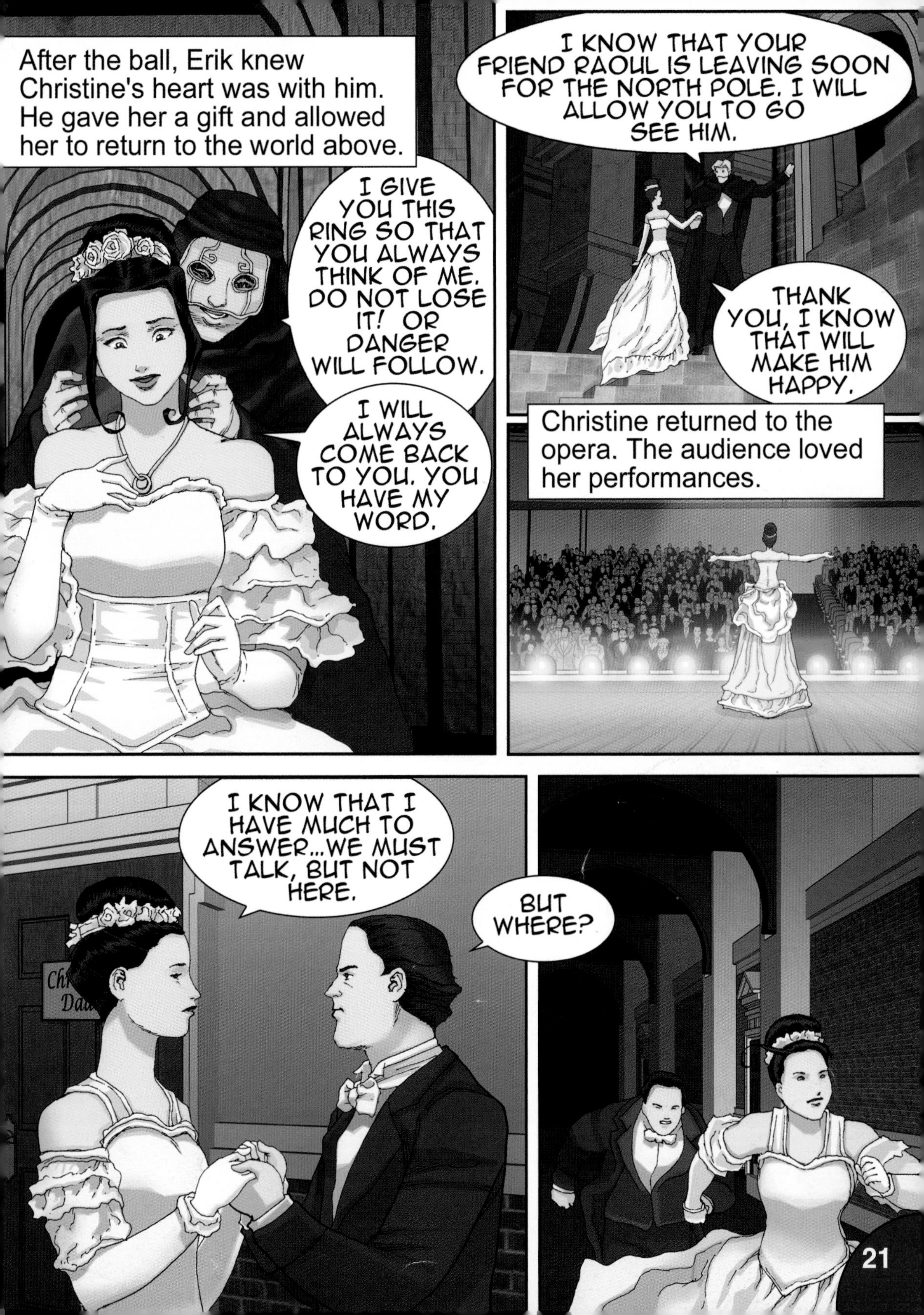
After the ball, Erik knew Christine's heart was with him. He gave her a gift and allowed her to return to the world above.
I GIVE YOU THIS RING SO THAT YOU ALWAYS THINK OF ME. DO NOT LOSE IT! OR DANGER WILL FOLLOW.
I WILL ALWAYS COME BACK TO YOU. YOU HAVE MY WORD.
I KNOW THAT YOUR FRIEND RAOUL IS LEAVING SOON FOR THE NORTH POLE. I WILL ALLOW YOU TO GO SEE HIM.
THANK YOU, I KNOW THAT WILL MAKE HIM HAPPY.
Christine returned to the opera. The audience loved her performances.
I KNOW THAT I HAVE MUCH TO ANSWER...WE MUST TALK, BUT NOT HERE.
BUT WHERE?

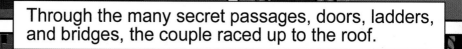

Through the many secret passages, doors, ladders, and bridges, the couple raced up to the roof.

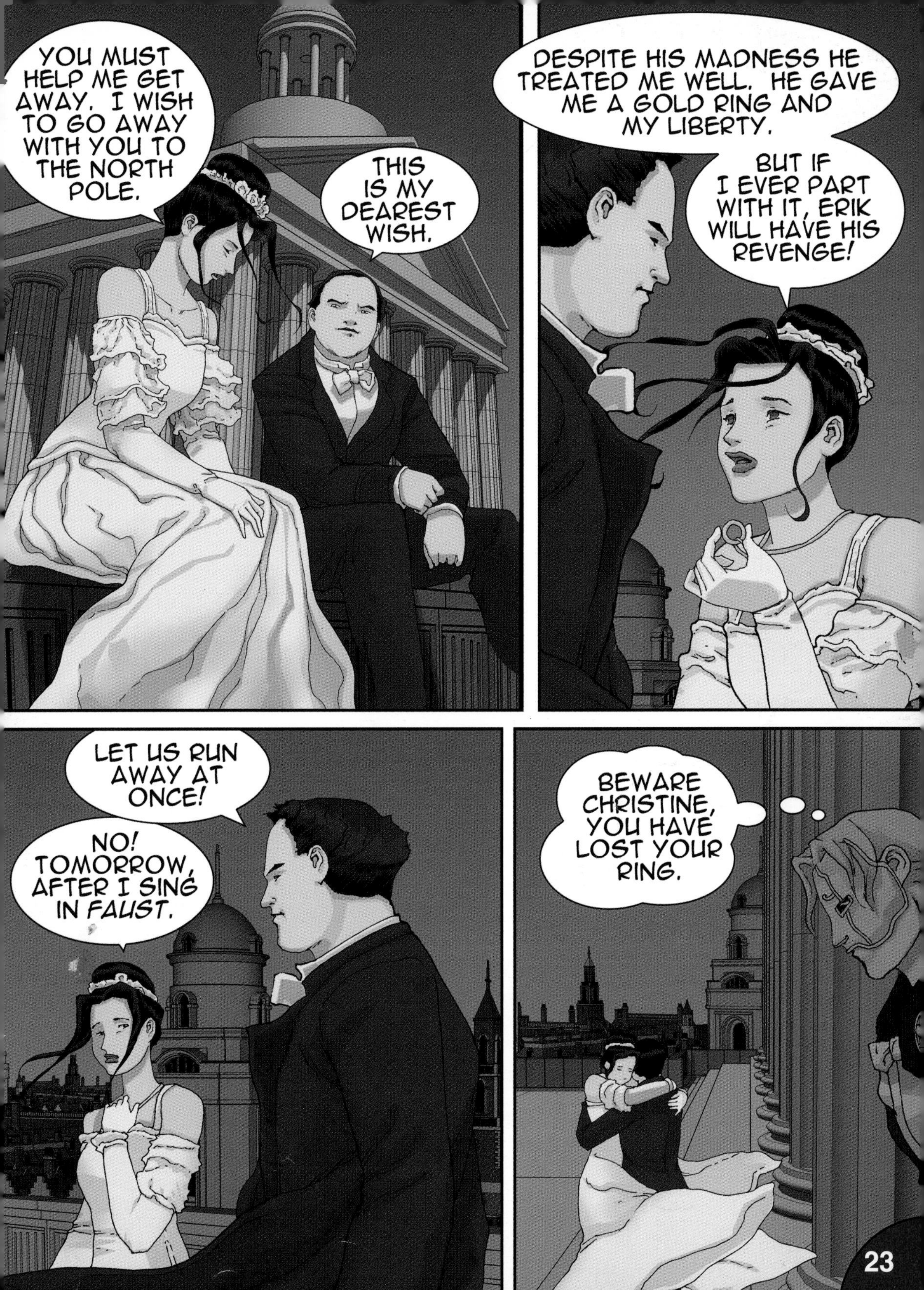
YOU MUST HELP ME GET AWAY. I WISH TO GO AWAY WITH YOU TO THE NORTH POLE.
THIS IS MY DEAREST WISH.
DESPITE HIS MADNESS HE TREATED ME WELL. HE GAVE ME A GOLD RING AND MY LIBERTY.
BUT IF I EVER PART WITH IT, ERIK WILL HAVE HIS REVENGE!
LET US RUN AWAY AT ONCE!
NO! TOMORROW, AFTER I SING IN *FAUST*.
BEWARE CHRISTINE, YOU HAVE LOST YOUR RING.

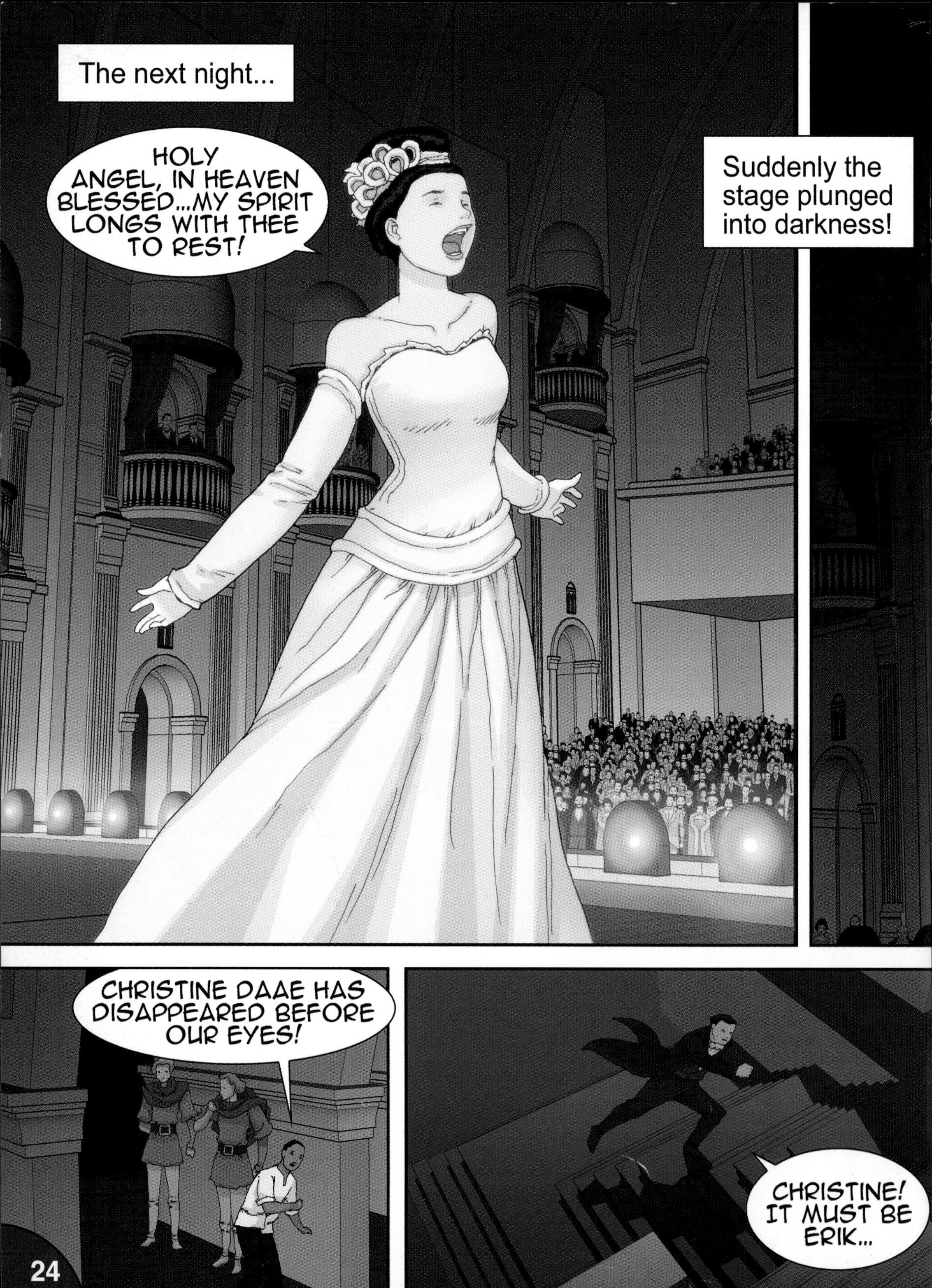

The next night...
HOLY ANGEL, IN HEAVEN BLESSED...MY SPIRIT LONGS WITH THEE TO REST!
Suddenly the stage plunged into darkness!
CHRISTINE DAAE HAS DISAPPEARED BEFORE OUR EYES!
CHRISTINE! IT MUST BE ERIK...

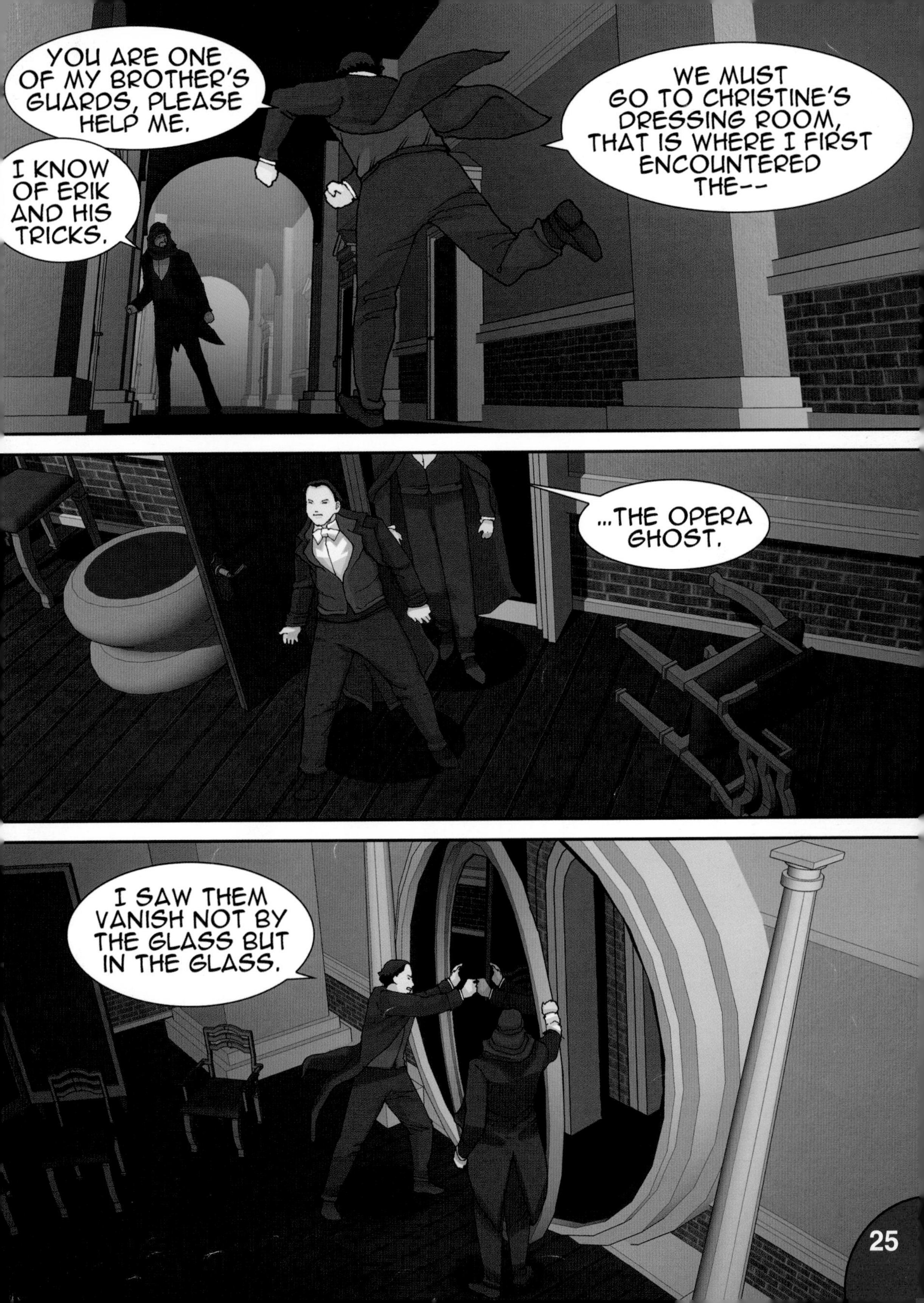
YOU ARE ONE OF MY BROTHER'S GUARDS, PLEASE HELP ME.
I KNOW OF ERIK AND HIS TRICKS.
WE MUST GO TO CHRISTINE'S DRESSING ROOM, THAT IS WHERE I FIRST ENCOUNTERED THE--
...THE OPERA GHOST.
I SAW THEM VANISH NOT BY THE GLASS BUT IN THE GLASS.

Behind the trapdoor they found dark passages and tunnels.
Finally, they reached a damp room covered in mirrors.
CHRISTINE! CHRISTINE!
RAOUL!
CHRISTINE! CAN YOU LET US OUT?
I DO NOT HAVE A KEY.
THE MONSTER HAD GIVEN ME UNTIL ELEVEN O'CLOCK TO MARRY HIM. IF I SAY NO EVERYBODY WILL BE BURIED UNDER THE RUINS OF THE PARIS GRAND OPERA!

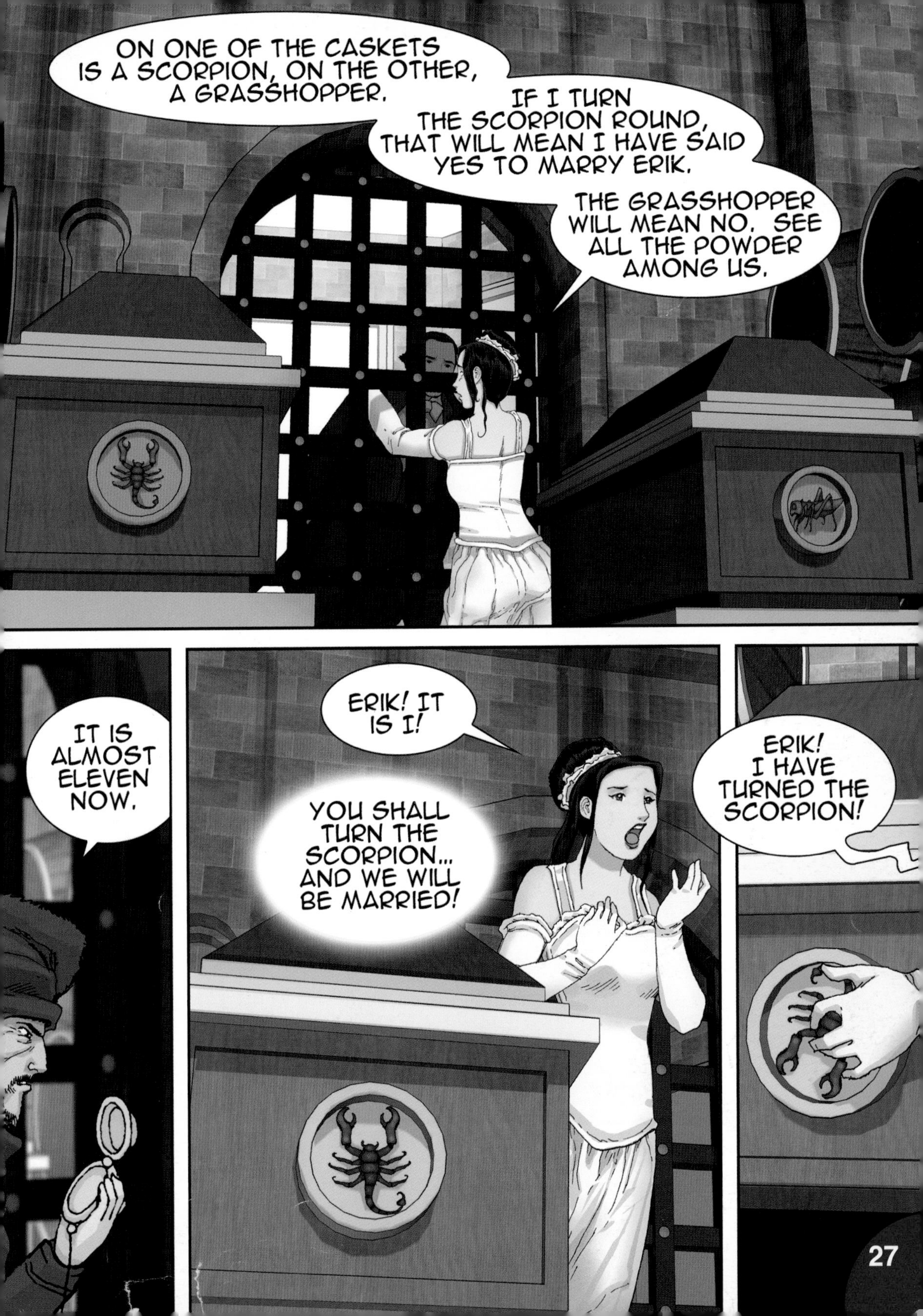
ON ONE OF THE CASKETS IS A SCORPION, ON THE OTHER, A GRASSHOPPER.
IF I TURN THE SCORPION ROUND, THAT WILL MEAN I HAVE SAID YES TO MARRY ERIK.
THE GRASSHOPPER WILL MEAN NO. SEE ALL THE POWDER AMONG US.
IT IS ALMOST ELEVEN NOW.
ERIK! IT IS I!
YOU SHALL TURN THE SCORPION... AND WE WILL BE MARRIED!
ERIK! I HAVE TURNED THE SCORPION!

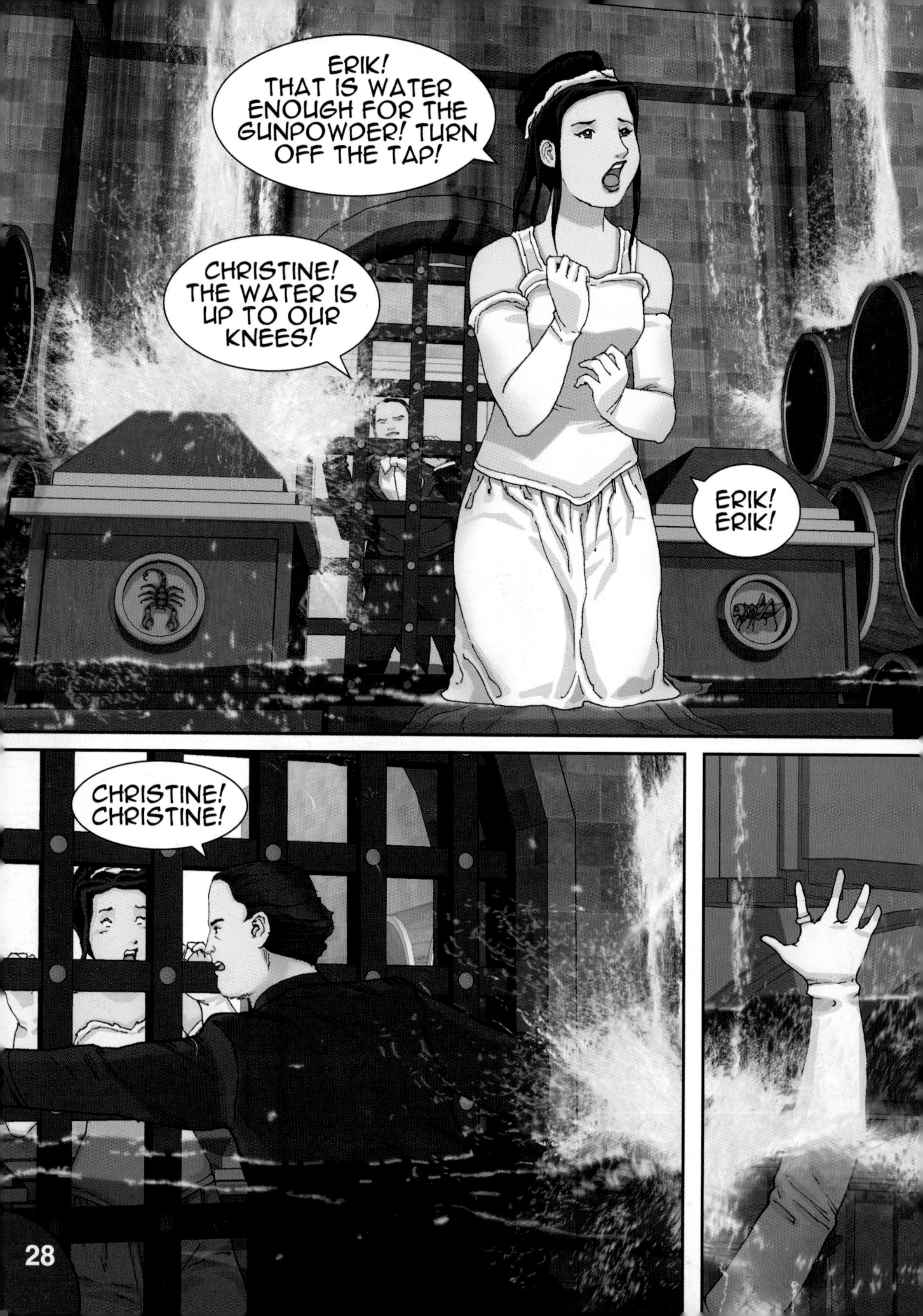
ERIK! THAT IS WATER ENOUGH FOR THE GUNPOWDER! TURN OFF THE TAP!
CHRISTINE! THE WATER IS UP TO OUR KNEES!
ERIK! ERIK!
CHRISTINE! CHRISTINE!

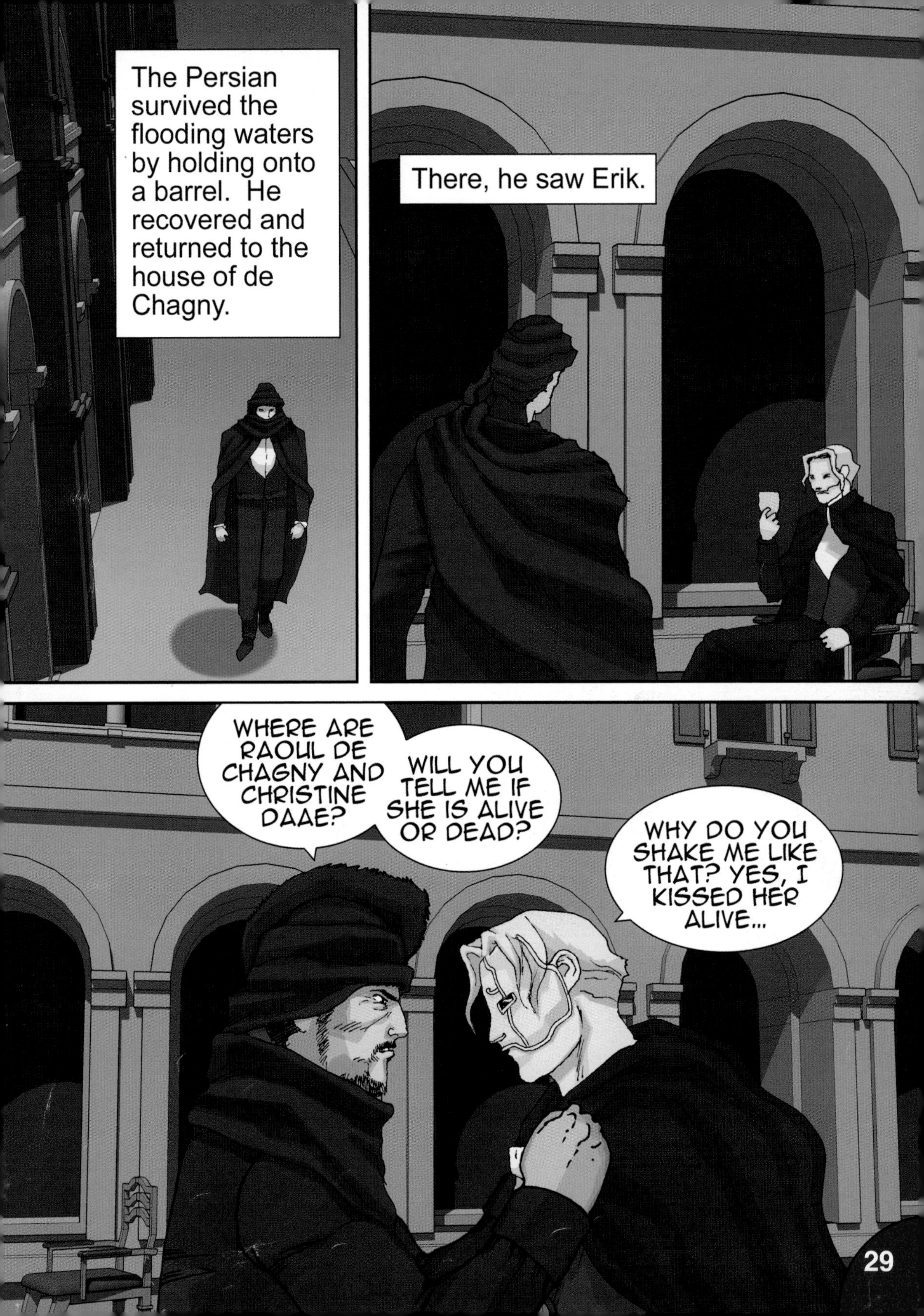
The Persian survived the flooding waters by holding onto a barrel. He recovered and returned to the house of de Chagny.
There, he saw Erik.
WHERE ARE RAOUL DE CHAGNY AND CHRISTINE DAAE?
WILL YOU TELL ME IF SHE IS ALIVE OR DEAD?
WHY DO YOU SHAKE ME LIKE THAT? YES, I KISSED HER ALIVE...

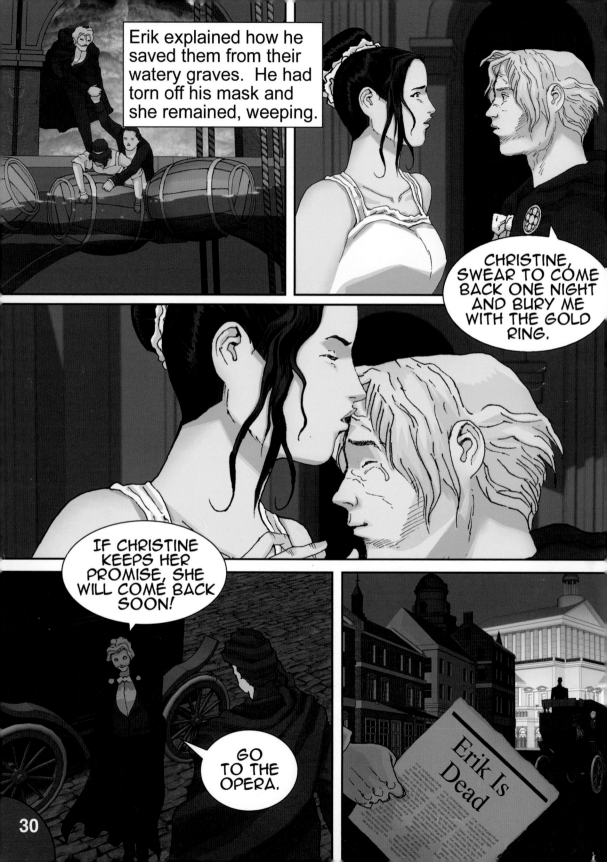

Erik explained how he saved them from their watery graves. He had torn off his mask and she remained, weeping.

CHRISTINE, SWEAR TO COME BACK ONE NIGHT AND BURY ME WITH THE GOLD RING.

IF CHRISTINE KEEPS HER PROMISE, SHE WILL COME BACK SOON!

GO TO THE OPERA.

Erik Is Dead

About the Author

Gaston Leroux was born in Paris, France, on May 6, 1868. After leaving school Leroux worked in a law office. He also began wiring essays and short stories in his free time.

By 1890, Leroux was working full-time as a journalist. He traveled the world from 1894 to 1906, reporting back to Paris. He also began writing novels. In 1907, his first success was *The Mystery of the Yellow Room*. Leroux wrote several sequels based on the main character, but none were as successful.

In 1911, *The Phantom of the Opera* was published as a novel. It received poor reviews and did not sell very well. Leroux continued to write and published several novels and plays, but he did not receive much recognition until 1925, when *The Phantom of the Opera* was filmed as a silent movie starring American actor Lon Chaney.

Gaston Leroux died in April 1927 in Nice, France. He did not achieve wide fame in his lifetime. However, *The Phantom of the Opera* gained renewed fame with Andrew Lloyd Webber's musical of the same name in 1986. In 2006, *Phantom* became the longest-running show in Broadway history.

Additional Works

The Mystery of the Yellow Room (1907)
The Phantom of the Opera (1911)
The Man with the Black Feather (1912)
The Secret of the Night (1914)
The Haunted Chair (1922)
Missing Men (1923)
The Machine to Kill (1924)
The Octopus of Paris (1926)

Glossary

allowance – money provided for personal or household expenses.

aristocrat – a person born into a high social class. Aristocrats run the government in some countries.

casket – a small chest or box.

masquerade – a party where people wear costumes and masks.

messieurs – plural for the French *monsieur*, meaning "mister."

Web Sites

To learn more about Gaston Leroux, visit the ABDO Group online at **www.abdopublishing.com**. Web sites about Leroux are featured on our Book Links page. These links are routinely monitored and updated to provide the most current information available.